Mary Abigail Roe

E. P. Roe

Reminiscences of his Life

Mary Abigail Roe

E. P. Roe
Reminiscences of his Life

ISBN/EAN: 9783337055646

Printed in Europe, USA, Canada, Australia, Japan

Cover: Foto ©Raphael Reischuk / pixelio.de

More available books at **www.hansebooks.com**

E. P. Roe

Reminiscences of his Life

By his Sister
Mary A. Roe

New York
Dodd, Mead and Company
1899

INTRODUCTORY NOTE.

SINCE the death of Edward Payson Roe, in 1888, there have been inquiries from time to time for some record of his life and work, and it is in response to these repeated requests that this volume is issued. While necessarily omitting much that is of too personal a nature for publication, the editor has allowed the subject of these Reminiscences to speak for himself as far as possible, although it has been thought advisable to introduce here and there various papers from outside sources that seem to throw additional light upon his character. It is believed that in this way a clearer picture may be given than would otherwise be obtained of the life of one who was, perhaps, the most popular American author of his generation. The editor's own part of the work has been confined to a simple statement of facts and to supplying connecting links, when such seemed needed, between the various letters and papers.

Thanks are due, and are hereby offered, to all who have kindly contributed material or in other ways assisted in the preparation of this volume.

CONTENTS

ILLUSTRATIONS

E. P. ROE

REMINISCENCES OF HIS LIFE

CHAPTER I

BOYHOOD AND COLLEGE DAYS

M Y brother Edward and I were the youngest of six children, and as he was my senior by but a few years we were playmates and almost inseparable companions in our childhood.

We were born in a roomy old-fashioned house, built by my mother's father for his oldest son, but purchased by my father when he retired from business in New York. A more ideal home for a happy childhood could not easily be found. It stood near the entrance of a beautiful valley through which flowed a clear stream, and was wind-sheltered by high bluffs, yet commanded fine views of the mountains with glimpses of the Hudson showing like lakes between them.

What we called the "side-hill," back of the house, was our chief playground. My brother delighted in climbing the hickory and chestnut trees that grew upon it, and it was here in spring that we searched for wild flowers, from the little hepaticas just peeping above the snow, to the laurel in its full glory. In after years Edward never visited the old home without a tramp to the top of that side-hill or along the wood-road at its base.

Our mother was always an invalid, and the housekeeper, Betsey Williams, who was a member of our family for many years, became like a second mother to us in her care and devotion. But she was no disciplinarian, and I have heard that when Edward was in a childish passion and she felt unable to cope with the situation she would pick him up bodily and carry him to my mother's couch. There he would sit beside her, not daring to move until he could promise obedience, held spellbound by the authority in her keen black eyes, though she was too weak to raise her hand to her head.

Edward's love of nature was inherited from both father and mother. Often, on lovely June days, he would draw mother's wheeled chair through the broad walks of our large square garden, where the borders on either side were gorgeous with flowers, while I gathered and piled the fragrant blossoms on her lap until she was fairly embowered. Yet one scarcely missed those that were plucked.

Back of the garden ran a clear brook, the overflow from a spring of soft, cool water at the base of the side-hill, and in it we often played and tumbled, soaking and soiling many a fresh clean suit.

As is usually the case with younger sisters, I always followed my brother's lead, and one summer day's adventure in particular stands clearly in my memory. We little children had started off with the avowed intention of looking for wild strawberries. We had secretly planned to visit the old house where my mother was born, which was some distance farther up the valley and at that time was unoccupied, but we thought it best not to make any announcement of this project in advance.

Edward had heard that in the cellar there was a stone vault in which our Grandfather Williams kept the money that General Washington had entrusted to his care until it was required to pay off the soldiers of the Revolution while they were encamped near Newburgh. Edward was eager to visit the cellar, thinking that possibly there might still be a few coins left. We entered the empty house by a back door and wandered through the rooms, he entertaining me the while with stories mother had told him of her childhood there.

Then we timidly groped our way down into the large cellar and found the stone vault — but it was filled only with cobwebs and dust!

When we came out and stood in the great kitchen Edward told me another Revolutionary story connected with the spot in our great-grandmother's day.

A company of British soldiers had been quartered upon the family, and the old kitchen swarmed with redcoats and negro servants, for those were still days of slavery in the North. Grandmother Brewster, who was a notable cook, had just placed in the heated brick oven a large baking of bread, pies, and cake. One of the soldiers asked her if they could have these good things provided they could take them away without her knowledge, but while she was in the kitchen. She, believing this impossible, said yes. He waited until everything was removed from the oven and placed upon a large table to cool. Suddenly a quarrel arose between several of the soldiers and one of her favorite colored boys. Fearing the lad would be killed she rushed into the midst of the crowd and at length succeeded in stopping the fight. When at last peace and quiet were restored, she turned round to find her morning's baking gone — and in a moment she understood the ruse they had practised upon her.

As Edward talked the whole story seemed very real to us, but when he had finished we walked up to the old oven, and looking into its cavernous depths he said: "*That's* here and the stone vault down cellar, but all those people are dead and gone. How strange and lonely it seems! Let's go."

Then we hurried off to a field near by which we called "the rose-patch." Not far from this spot stood formerly an old mill where snuff was manufactured, and the rose-bushes that in bygone days had yielded their blossoms to scent the snuff were still living and flowering. But among the roses was an abundance of wild strawberries, and the two children soon lost all thoughts of the past in their enjoyment of the luscious fruit. But the old deserted house with its Revolutionary associations never ceased to have great attractions for us. Across the road from it, and nearer the creek, was a mound of cinders marking the spot where once stood the forge upon which our grandfather wrought the great iron chain which was stretched across the Hudson for the purpose of keeping British ships from sailing beyond it. Some links of this chain are now kept as relics in the Washington "Headquarters" at Newburgh.

In later years Edward planned to write a story entitled "The Fair Captives of Brooklyn Heights," embodying some incidents in the lives of our Grandfather Williams' sisters, who lived there with their widowed mother. During the Revolution a number of British officers installed themselves at her house, and the old lady promptly locked up her daughters in order to prevent any possible love-making. One of the girls eluded her vigilance, however, married an officer, and fled with him to Canada. She returned after the war was over, but her mother, who had never forgiven the deception, refused to receive her, and she and her husband went to England to live.

In our home at Moodna was always to be found a generous hospitality. Among our most loved and honored guests was Dr. Samuel Cox, who was for many years a prominent clergyman in New York and Brooklyn. My father had been a member of his church and they were lifelong friends. Often, in summer, he and his family spent weeks at a time with us, and we children, as well as our elders, were always charmed listeners to his conversation. He had a fine memory, and it was remarkably well stored with classic poetry. Sometimes he would entertain us with selections from the "Iliad," but more often, when other guests were present and Edward and I were seated on the piazza steps, on warm moonlight evenings, he would repeat whole cantos from "Marmion" or "Lady of the Lake," or perhaps some fine passages from "Paradise Lost."

At times the conversation would turn upon ancient history, and I remember on one occasion he asked Edward and me if we could give him the names of the first Roman triumvirate. At this period of our existence the name "Cæsar" was associated exclusively with an old colored man whom we often visited and who lived upon a lonely road which is still called "Cæsar's Lane." We were vastly astonished, therefore, to learn that the name had ever been borne by any more illustrious personage than our dusky friend. But we listened, entranced, while the doctor told of the rivalries and conflicts of those two great generals, Cæsar and Pompey, for the empire of the world. He could not remember the name of the third triumvir, and it troubled him greatly. That night, about two o'clock, I was startled by a loud knock at my bedroom door, and Dr. Cox called out, "Mary, are you awake?" I replied that I was — as, indeed, was every one else in the house by that time. "It's Crassus," he said, then returned to his room greatly relieved that he had finally recalled the name. Edward and I never forgot our first lesson in Roman History.

This learned clergyman was often very absent-minded. During one of his visits to us he had been for a drive with his wife and our mother. On their return he stopped at the horse-block, near where Edward and I were playing, threw down the reins, and, engrossed in some train of

thought, walked into the house, utterly forgetful
of the ladies on the back seat.   They, very much
amused, continued their conversation and waited
to see if he would remember them.   Finally, however, as he did not reappear, Edward was called to
assist them from the carriage and unharness the
horse.   Some time afterward the doctor rushed
out of the front door and around the house, having
just remembered where he left the companions of
his drive.

The first school Edward and I attended was a
private one for boys and girls kept by our eldest
brother Alfred, in the village of Canterbury, two
miles distant from our home.   We trudged over
the hills together on pleasant days and drove
over when the weather was stormy.   I well remember the abnormal interest we felt in the
health of an aunt of ours who lived near the
school and who had some fine fruit trees on her
place.   After our inquiries in regard to her welfare had been answered she was sure to invite us
to examine the ground beneath those trees, while
the merry twinkle in her eyes showed appreciation
of the fact that our devotion to her was not altogether disinterested.

Of my brother's later school and college days,
the Rev. A. Moss Merwin, now of Pasadena, Cali
fornia, writes : —

" It was at Cornwall-on-the-Hudson I first met Edward, a fellow student in his brother Alfred's classical school. His face and manners were attractive, and intellectually he ranked high among his companions. Well informed as to current events, with a wider knowledge of books than is usual with young men of his years, and with great facility in expressing his thoughts orally and in writing, he commanded our respect from the first. And when we saw from time to time articles from his pen in the New York *Evangelist* descriptive of stirring events, our respect grew into admiration for him who was *facile princeps* in our small literary world. Then as we came to know something of his kindness of heart and enthusiasm for the good and true we loved him.

" His particular friends among the boarding pupils enjoyed the privilege of being invited occasionally to the hospitable home of his parents. What a home it was! Abundant comfort without ostentation or luxury. The father a retired business man, kindly, philanthropic, and an ardent lover of plants and flowers. The mother an invalid in her wheeled chair, a woman with sunshine in eye and voice, of unusual intelligence, highly cultivated, with charming conversational powers.

" In the little Presbyterian church near the school, planted mainly through the exertions of his father and elder brothers, there came a time of special religious interest when Edward was deeply impressed. With loving purpose he sought out two of his most intimate companions, and through his instrumentality they then began the Christian life. One became a successful business man in Chicago, and to the day of his death remembered with gratitude the helping hand and earnest words of E. P. Roe. The other friend remembers that soon after that decision, when he and Edward were walking through the grounds of the Friends' meeting-house, they covenanted together to study for the ministry.

"We were together again preparing for college at Burr and Burton Seminary, Manchester, Vermont. How enthusiastic he was over the beautiful scenery of that now far-famed summer resort in the Green Mountains! How delighted to send his father a present through his own earnings by sawing several cords of wood!"

About this time our father's property in New York City was destroyed by fire, and owing to the expense of rebuilding he was obliged for a time to practise close economy. But fortunately it was not found necessary to take any of his children from school or college. To quote Mr. Merwin further: —

"At Williams College we saw much of each

E. P. ROE AS A STUDENT.

other. Roe was a fair scholar, more intent at getting at the meaning of the text, and its mythological and historical relations, than in making what is called a fair recitation. His ability as a writer and speaker was recognized early in his college course when elected speaker of his class at a Washington's Birthday banquet. Friends he easily made, and with many remained in pleasant relations to the close of his life. Trouble with his eyes caused him to shorten his course at college, but the authorities, in view of his subsequent success as a writer, gave him his diploma."

My brother excelled in athletic sports in his youth, particularly in swimming and skating. On one occasion when he was home on vacation, he and a young companion were skating on the river. His friend, who was skimming along in advance of him, suddenly fell into an air-hole and sank out of sight. Edward instantly realized that if he went to the spot to rescue him, he also would break through. With quick presence of mind, therefore, he unwound a long worsted muffler from his neck and threw one end of it into the opening. As soon as the struggling boy rose to the surface, Edward shouted, "Take hold of that tippet and I'll pull you out!" His friend did as he was directed and Edward, by exerting all his strength, succeeded in drawing him out of the water and upon the solid ice, fortunately not much the worse for his immersion.

Adjoining our father's property was that of Mr. Nathaniel Sands, a " Friend " and a gentleman in all that the words imply, who was loved and respected by the whole community. His residence commanded an extended view of the river and mountains and especially of the narrow Gap of the Highlands. At his death the old homestead became the summer residence of his eldest son, Dr. David Sands, the head of a well-known firm of druggists in New York.

While my brother was at the theological seminary, and just about the beginning of the Civil War, he became engaged to Dr. Sands' second daughter, Anna. The young people had known each other from childhood, and this happy culmination of their long friendship was not unexpected by either family.

CHAPTER II

LIFE AS CHAPLAIN

ONE of Edward's schoolmates at Cornwall, writing of him, said : "We met again on a most memorable evening in the early days of the war, when with two young ladies, one of whom became his wife, we rowed out on the Hudson River, under the shadow of Storm King, while the whole sky from west to east flamed with crimson-tinted clouds, that seemed a portent of the scenes to follow. When we reached the dock on our return the evening papers brought the details of the battle of Bull Run, fought on the previous day."

I remember Edward's intense excitement on his return home that night, and his remark that if he were only through his seminary course he would join the army as chaplain. From that time I believe the purpose was constantly in his mind; and the next year, 1862, although his studies were not then completed, he became chaplain of the famous Harris Light Cavalry, under the command of the gallant Kilpatrick, later Brigadier and Major General, who was always my brother's firm friend.

The following testimony to Edward's work among the soldiers was written upon the field by a correspondent of the New York *Tribune*.

" Chaplain Roe, of the Second New York (Harris Light) Cavalry, is a man whose praises are in the mouth of every one for timely and efficient services. He is always with the regiment, and his whole time is devoted to the temporal and spiritual welfare of the men. He is their friend, adviser, and counsellor, and commands the respect of all who know him — something that cannot be said of every chaplain in the army."

The *Observer* of that year also published a letter written by a private in the Harris Light Cavalry to his parents. In it is found this reference to their chaplain.

" To-day is Sunday, and, as a great exception, it has appeared like Sunday. This morning we had service at headquarters, the chaplain of our regiment officiating, and I think I can safely call him a pious army chaplain, which I cannot say of any others that *I* ever knew; and notwithstanding the little respect most chaplains have shown to them, and still less encouragement, this one, by his mild, gentle, manly, humble, and Christian-like demeanor, has won the respect of all with whom he has had intercourse, from the most profane and vulgar to the most gentlemanly, which few chaplains have been able to do. In a fight he is seen encouraging the men; in the hospital administering to the soldier's wants, both spiritually and bodily. Last winter, during the worst days of a Virginia winter, I have seen him going from camp to camp, distributing his books and papers; and with his own earnings he would buy delicacies that a poor sick soldier would otherwise in vain long for. These and other innumerable like acts have gradually caused every one to at least respect him, and some to love him. His name is Rev. E. P. Roe, Chaplain Harris Light Cavalry. I have been informed that he had just graduated when he came into the army. I think Dr. P—— may know him. I believe he is a Presbyterian. If you had any idea what a chaplain had to contend with, in order to lead a consistent life, you might then understand why I speak so of him. S."

While with this regiment Edward acted as weekly correspondent for the New York *Evangelist*. A few of his letters to that paper are here reprinted, in the hope that they may still be found of interest. They are characteristic of the writer and give a clearer idea of his life at this time than can be obtained in any other way.

"CAMP HALL'S HILL, Oct. 15, 1862.

" MESSRS. EDITORS: — Till within a few days past we have been enjoying splendid weather, days as warm and sunny as those of June, and moonlight nights so clear and beautiful that one could sit at his tent door and read ordinary type with perfect ease and pleasure. Of course we improved such favourable weather and held our prayer-meetings nearly every night. I shall never forget one religious service that we had last week.

"As usual a large fire was kindled in front of the chaplain's tent, and the men, having disposed of their suppers, were beginning to assemble. Soon the musical " church-call " sounded to hasten the lagging ones, and by the time our exercises commenced about two hundred were present. Our meetings are of a free and general character, open to all who are willing to take part in them. We commence by singing two or three hymns or patriotic songs in succession, the sound of music calling the men together. A prayer is then offered, after which I endeavor by some anecdote or illustration to force home the truth and necessity of a Saviour upon the minds of those present. The Christian members of the regiment then follow in prayer, singing, and exhortation, till we are dispersed by the roll-call. We have interruptions in this, our usual programme, of such a nature, and with such frequency, that we have great reason to be thankful and encouraged. They are occasioned by the stepping forth of soldiers in front of the fire who have hitherto been silent in our meetings, and who either ask the prayers of Christians that they may be led to the Saviour, or calmly and firmly state their intention to enlist under the banner of the Cross, and urge their comrades to do likewise.

"Towards the close of the service I have mentioned, three young men rose up together, and calmly and firmly one after another stated their resolution, with God's help, to live a Christian life. O that some of our cold, half-hearted professors could have been here then. Would to God that the voices of those young soldiers, as they urged with simple and earnest eloquence their comrades to come to the Saviour likewise, might be heard throughout all the churches of the North, and sound in every prayer-meeting, in our land. Such earnest tones and words would soon disperse the moral and religious apathy that seems to reign undisturbed in many localities, for they would prove that the Spirit of God was present. It was a scene that would have moved the coldest heart, and stirred the most sluggish nature. The starry sky, the full moon overhead flooding all the landscape with the softest and most beautiful radiance, the white tents covering the hillsides, the large fire blazing fitfully up, surrounded by two hundred or more men who might readily be taken at first glance to be a band of Spanish brigands, all conspired to make a picture that any artist would wish to copy. But as you listened to the words of those young men, and the earnest prayer and songs of praise that followed, all such fanciful thoughts of banditti and romance would melt away, and the strange, peculiar costume of those present would become simply the ordinary dress that the rude taste or necessity of the men during their campaign had led them to assume, and the dark-bearded faces, made still more sombre and sinister by the partial light, would resolve themselves into the bronzed honest features of our American soldiers, now expressive of solemn thought and feeling. Never was a sound more unwelcome and discordant than the roll-call which broke up that assembly.

"After the roll-call a group generally lingers around the fire, and I often find in it those who wish to be spoken with on the subject of religion. So it happened this night. A soldier chanced to be passing by our encampment, and, attracted by the sound of music, stopped at our meeting. A few days before he had received a letter from home stating that his mother was very ill and not expected to live many days. He knew he should never see her again, and his heart was tender and sad. Thus prepared for the truth by the Providence of God, his steps were directed to us, and as he sat there and listened to those three young men as they stated their resolution from thenceforth to serve God, he too resolved to be a Christian, and has since found peace in believing. I told him how our prayer-meeting had been started by two or three Christian soldiers meeting openly for prayer, and that the same happy state of things might be brought about in his regiment in a similar manner. He promised that the prayer-meeting should be commenced.

"The 18th of this month (October) was as beautiful and bright a Sabbath morning as ever dawned on Virginia. Though the day and all nature spoke of peace, yet men would not hearken, for it was soon evident that our brief repose was again to be broken. The Third Division of cavalry was encamped on the northwestern edge of the old Bull Run battlefield. The day before we occupied the battlefield itself. The earlier part of the day was spent by the different regiments in preparing to march, and by noon the concentration of the entire command began. Distant outposts, regiments on picket, and scouting parties were drawn in, and soon after the battle-flags of General Kilpatrick, General Davies, and General Custer were seen fluttering through forests or over hills in the direction of the Warrenton and Alexandria pike. Following them were long lines of cavalry and artillery, and above all, a bright October sun that gave to the scene anything but the grimness of war. As evening approached we came out on Warrenton pike. General Davies' brigade had the advance, and part of the Harris Light Cavalry was thrown out as skirmishers. It soon struck the enemy's pickets, and then a running fight was kept up until within a short distance of Gainesville. Our flying artillery took advantage of every high position to send a shell shrieking after the enemy. It was now dark night. The head of our column had advanced up within a short distance of the point where the railroad crossed the pike before entering the village. For a short time there had been an ominous silence on the part of the rebels, and it became necessary to send forward part of the Harris Light Cavalry to find what had become of them. The detachment moved on to cross the railroad embankment, when suddenly, from over its top, at a given signal, a line of fire at least three hundred yards long flashed out into the night, and a perfect storm of bullets rained over their heads. Fortunately the enemy fired too high to do much execution, and only a few were wounded. Our boys returned the volley, and then retired to a small piece of woods, and for a time a hot skirmish was maintained. Having no knowledge of the force that might be concealed in the place, and the position being too strong to be carried by a night assault, further operations were deferred till morning. The 1st Virginia were left on picket close to the enemy and the rest of the command fell somewhat back and went into camp.

" To one not familiar with army life in the field, our mode of encamping that night would have been extremely interesting and suggestive. We were in the face of the enemy, which is no place for careless security. Each brigade was placed by itself, supporting the batteries which were put in position ready to be used at a moment's notice. The horses of each regiment were drawn up in ranks and tied to stakes driven into the ground for the purpose. Each man slept at the head of his horse, which he kept saddled, and part of the time bridled. Within three minutes the entire division could have been out in line of battle. I have known our regiment to saddle their horses, lead out from the woods, form ranks, count four and stand ready to charge into anything that might oppose, within just three minutes by the watch. In the rear of this warlike array the ammunition wagons and ambulances were parked in regular

order, the team horses standing ready harnessed.
Thus Kilpatrick's little fighting division lay there
that night like a panther crouched ready to spring.
During the night wagons came up with rations,
which were soon distributed. The groupings
around the fires, after this, were picturesque in
the extreme. Some of the men, shrouded in their
great military overcoats, stood quietly warming
themselves, throwing out immense shadows that
stretched away till lost in the surrounding darkness. The dusky forms of others might be seen
passing to and fro in the preparation of their rude
meal of fried pork and hardtack, while the flickering blaze revealed the burly forms of a still greater
number reposing upon the ground in all varieties
of attitude. At last the entire division, except the
vigilant pickets and sentinels, was wrapped in
slumber. At four o'clock the bugle sounded
reveille, and the camp was soon all astir. Soon
after we saw a flash in the direction of the enemy,
and listened breathlessly a moment for the report
of rebel cannon, but the long interval and distant
heavy rumble that followed satisfied us that a
storm other than that of war was about to break
over us; and soon it came, with high cold winds
and drenching rain. As we cowered around our
smoking, dying fires in the dim twilight of that
wild October morning — ah! then we thought of

being tucked away in snug feather-beds under the
old roof-tree at home; but there was no repining,
though we all knew that on the coming night
many would sleep colder than ever before — so
cold that nothing but the breath of God could
give warmth again.

"But we were not long left to reflection of any
kind, for regiment after regiment now began to
take position upon the line of march. General
Custer's brigade had the advance. Soon scattering shots and an occasional boom of a cannon told
us that we had again found the enemy. But no
stand was made until we reached Broad Run, and
there the firing became rapid and sharp. Our
brigade now came up and was placed in position, and the battle became general. Every now
and then a shell would whiz over our heads and
explode, inspiring anything but agreeable emotions. Several charges were made on both sides.
I wonder if it is possible to give any idea of a
rebel charge. Their cries and yells are so peculiar, so wild, shrill, feverish, so ghastly (I had
almost said ghostly), for the sounds seem so unreal, more like horrid shrieks heard in a dream
than the utterances of living men. The shouting
of our men is deeper and hoarser, and partakes
more of the chest tone in its character, but the
rebels charge with a yell that is something be-

tween the shriek of a woman and the scream of a
panther. At times you can close your eyes and
imagine that some fierce conflict of another age is
passing before you in a dream, so strange and unnatural does it seem to see men engaged in mortal
combat. We finally dislodged the enemy from
their very strong position and advanced across
Broad Run. General Custer took a strong position
on a hill above the stream, while General Davies
was ordered with his brigade to advance as far as
possible toward Warrenton, for General Kilpatrick
had received written orders to move out as far as
he could upon this road in order to discover the
force and intentions of the enemy. The surgeons
and ambulances halted in a field between the two
brigades. I stayed with them, and was trying to
get a feed for my horse, which was evidently beginning to feel the effects of long marches and short
rations, when suddenly I heard firing nearly opposite us, on our left flank. At first I thought it
was a mere skirmish with some rebels left in the
woods and discovered by our men; but the firing
became more rapid every moment, and soon General Custer's battery began to shell the woods
most vigorously. I saw that the woods were full
of men, but could not distinguish ours from the
rebels. Two or three aids galloped by in the
direction General Davies had taken.

"One remarked in passing, with an ominous look and shake of his head, ' You had better be getting out of here,' which was not a very comforting suggestion to those who had no orders to ' get out of here ' or where to get to. It was very evident that something was wrong, and that matters were getting serious. Wagon and ambulance drivers, surgeons and their attendants, contrabands with their led horses — in short, all of us — were like a covey of startled quails, their heads up, aware of danger, but not knowing which way to fly. We could not very well show fight, for a charge by a wagon train would be almost as great a novelty as General Kilpatrick's' attacking gunboats with cavalry, which he actually did last summer on the Rappahannock, and destroyed them, too. But we, not at all envious, were glad to receive orders to retrace our steps; for nothing is so uncomfortable for a soldier as to hear firing in his rear. We were proceeding leisurely and in good order, when an orderly rode rapidly up to our front and turned us off on a by-road through the woods, with an injunction to move rapidly and come out on the main pike near Gainesville. Away we went in the direction of Thoroughfare Gap, the wagons banging and bouncing over stones and stumps, through streams and mudholes, as we followed the sinuosities of a narrow wood-road which finally led into the open fields. Here I felt like crying and laughing both — crying with rage at what I then considered our disgraceful retreat; but when I afterwards learned what odds we were contending against, I was satisfied that the best generalship was displayed in rapid retreat. And gravity itself would have laughed at the figure we cut. Contrabands and camp followers were careering by in all states of panic. Many had lost their hats in coming through the woods, and it seemed in some cases now that their wool fairly stood upon end, while they, rolling their eyes over their shoulders in the direction of the enemy, exhibited only their whites to the observer in front. Here might be seen an unfortunate darkie hauling on a stubborn mule that with its wonted perversity wanted to turn around and run the other way; there a man trying to raise a horse that had fallen with him ; while ' Git up, dar; git up, I tell yer,' resounded from every side. Some poor mules and some led horses fairly got frantic, for what with the beating they received, and with tin kettles rattling and captured chickens cackling between their legs, it was enough to distract any brute; so they kicked and floundered till they burst their girths, and galloped away rejoicing in their freedom. But the comic was soon lost in the tragic. The pursuing enemy was now closing upon us from all sides. The rear guard, which was the Harris Light Cavalry, made many a gallant stand, but what could a few men do against twenty times their number? With many it became a sad race for life and liberty. But before dusk we had the satisfaction of effectually checking the enemy. For the first time in my life I found myself rallying a body of men in a fight. Officers and men coming in rapidly, we soon had a respectable line formed and the enemy's advance was now decidedly checked. Captain Elder, who had brought off all his guns in safety, planted them on an eminence, and soon they were thundering defiance to the baffled enemy. Shell after shell screamed over our heads and exploded. Soon after a part of the First Corps came up, formed a line of battle, and relieved our thinned and wearied ranks. We retired to the friendly shelter of a neighbouring forest, and that deep sleep which follows great excitement and exertion quietly stretched us out as motionless and unconscious seemingly as the lifeless forms of our brave comrades that lay cold and stark along the line of our bloody retreat."

" Many changes and much marching and counter-marching have taken place since the soldiers of the Harris Light Cavalry gathered nightly under

the old apple tree, or in front of the chaplain's
tent, during the warm moonlight evenings of September and October.   The rich autumn foliage
that then made even poor old desolated Virginia
look beautiful has dropped away, and stern winter, rendered all the more grim and forbidding ·by
the ravages of war, now reigns supreme.   Many
of our number, also, like the leaves, have dropped
away.   Some, having obtained and squandered
their bounty, have treacherously deserted and
sneaked away like thievish hounds.   The bullet,
accident, and sickness have each conspired to
lessen our number, and many a noble-hearted fellow who was always first and foremost in all a
soldier's duty is now languishing in some hospital,
or sleeping beneath the sod that last sleep from
which no bugle call shall waken him.

" It seems as if God was teaching us to look to
himself, and not to men, for among those that
sickness has for the present removed from our
number were three who were the very stay and
central pillars of our regimental church.   Especially do I feel the loss of Brother Farber, who
was as noble a specimen of a Christian soldier as
it has ever been my fortune to meet.   Uniting
culture of heart and mind with a happy disposition, a shrewd and quick perception of character,
and a manner that made him popular with all, he

was just such an ally as the chaplain needed in
the ranks. Though he made his religion respected
by all, he also made it attractive, and his society
was not shunned, even by the wildest spirits of the
regiment. His cheerful smile and words were
better than medicine in the hospital, and I almost
always found him there when off duty. Nearly
two months ago he left us for a hospital in Washington, sick with the typhoid fever, contracted
doubtless by over-fatigue in his care of the sick
and bodies of the deceased, and by breathing air
tainted with disease. I have since received a
letter from him stating that he was very sick, and
that the surgeon said it would be months before
he could join the regiment again, if ever. For
aught I know his warfare may now be over and he
at rest, for I have received no answer to my reply
to his letter. Brothers Vernon and Stillwell are
also away sick. Only pastors, and they not fully,
can realize the loss that such men are to a chaplain. He has so few capable, warm-hearted co-
adjutors in a regiment as a general thing. There
is such a torrent of evil influences rushing in on
every side, that he sorely feels the need of men
possessing firm and established Christian characters, who would quietly and consistently stand up
for, and live religion on all occasions. Here he
has none of the conventionalities and restraints of

society to aid him, and even the heavenly influence of Christian parents, of pure sisters, and loving wives is weakened by distance, absence, and sin. But in grappling with the many and powerful demoralizing influences and vices of camp life, one soon learns that but little can be accomplished except by the direct aid and interposition of the Holy Spirit, for nothing short of the grace of God can enable the soldier to resist the evil that assails him on every side.

"While I was on a brief business visit to the North, the regiment had joined the advance, and on my return I found it out in the neighborhood of Warrenton. After waiting a few days in what remained of our old camp, I found an opportunity of going out to the front with Captain Cook, of our regiment, and a small squad of men. The ride out to Rappahannock Station, where our regiment was last heard from, was full of novelty and interest to one who had never been on a long march before. Captain Cook is a gentleman as well as a good soldier, and his familiarity with the historic region through which we passed made him an exceedingly agreeable companion. The evening of the second day of our journey, which was Sunday, found us considerably beyond Manassas. A dismantled house stood on the brow of a hill in a grove some distance from the road. We rode up to it and concluded to spend the night there. Though it was half ruin- ous, without windows and doors, and the floor covered with rubbish of every description, but a few moments sufficed to make it sufficiently com- fortable for a soldier's purpose. A fire blazing on the hearth, the rubbish cleared away, a blanket hung over the windows and doors, made our night quarters complete. Then gathering around the fire, each broiled his slip of bacon on the end of a stick, and enjoyed this rude repast far better than many a well appointed banquet in the North, for 'hunger was our sauce.' After supper we had, as it were, family prayers. The old dilapidated man- sion, the costume, arms, and varied expressions of the soldiers as they lounged around listening to the Word of God, all brought into view by the flickering blaze that roared within the chimney, made a scene that any artist might wish to copy.

" After marching all the next day we joined our wagon train at dusk, near Rappahannock Station, and found that we were just in time, for the whole army was on the move to Fredericksburg. Join- ing the train, I marched half the night with them in the darkness and rain. As there was no shelter near, the next day was spent in the rain under a tree; and an attack on the wagon train being ex- pected on the following night, my slumbers were neither very sound nor long continued. But such is the wonderful vitality that life in the open air gives, that one soon recovers from loss of sleep and fatigue. Our regiment moved down to Brook's Station, where it remained doing picket duty till it joined the advance on Fredericksburg.

"Our brigade, with our beloved and lamented General Bayard in command, was drawn up on a hillside preparatory to marching, and I assure you that the long lines and dense masses of cavalry made a splendid and imposing appearance. It was nearly night before we filed off towards Falmouth. The night was dark and misty and the roads broken and wild. Sometimes we would plunge down into a deep gully, at others scramble up the slippery and frozen sides of a steep hill. Every now and then horse and rider would be down, to the great merriment of all witnesses. But the joke became too serious when a horse fell and broke one poor fellow's leg.

"Seen through the mist and darkness, the long extended column, winding among the broken hills, now coming out in bold relief on the brow of one of them, and then descending again into the valley or the gloom of some forest, had a shadowy and phantom-like appearance, and seemed more like a procession in a dream than a goodly number of well armed troopers on a march. Especially was this spectral effect heightened when a distant part of the column would pass within the lurid glare of some brilliant camp-fire. After floundering through streams and quagmires, and filing through gorges that reminded one of the old Indian ambuscades, we turned off into a forest to encamp for the night. Selecting a tree from under which the snow had partially melted away, a few of us built a fire, then spread our blankets and slept on the ground in the clear, frosty starlight as well as on the softest couch our limbs had ever pressed. Long before daylight, the bugle sounded ' boots and saddles,' and the woods soon resounded with the customary martial clamor of an encampment.

"Suddenly every sound was hushed, for the distant boom of the two guns that opened the battle of Fredericksburg broke upon our ears. The silence was succeeded by wild shouts of enthusiasm, and soon we were on our way to the scene of action. The sharp rattle of musketry now began to mingle with the report of cannon. As we approached the river the roar of the artillery was truly grand and awful. I can only compare it to a very violent thunder-storm, wherein you hear, at one and the same time, the rumble and mutter of some peal dying away in the distance, the heavy, jarring roll more near, and the loud stunning explosion from the flash overhead. Our cavalry was crowded on a plain in the rear of our batteries. We did not know that the rebels were not replying to our guns, and expected every minute they would get our range. As we remained undisturbed, I concluded that our distance from the river was much greater than I had first supposed; but when the order came to march, and we filed off, by twos, down towards the river, past our batteries, I expected every moment to see the head of our column broken and shattered by shot and shell. I have heard much about "lazy soldiers and large pay," but I thought at that time that the soldier who marches steadily and determinedly forward on such occasions earns in five minutes all the pay he ever gets. But the heavy cannonading was only from our own guns, for the rebels were reserving their fire. We soon found that our orders were not to cross, but to go down the river and do picket duty on the extreme left flank. As we marched along, a shell from one of our batteries on a hill above me passed directly over my head. As it hissed by, it gave me an idea of the infinitely short space of time in which many of our poor boys are dashed into eternity.

"The early dawn of Saturday morning saw us returning to the battlefield. About nine o'clock we mounted the hill, and formed upon the plain on the opposite side of the river. As we were taking our position, I heard a whizzing sound, and saw the earth torn up by a solid shot quite near me. They soon screamed over our heads and fell all around us; but, as a general thing, the enemy fired too high. A few hundred yards to our front, the shells were bursting constantly. We remained on the plain all that day and night, the fire in front of us sometimes slackening, and sometimes ceasing altogether. We often cast anxious glances at some rebel batteries quite near us on the right, and often wondered why they did not open upon us, for if they did, they could have swept us from the plain in a few moments. Either our batteries occupied them, or they reserved their fire for some purpose. A little after noon, we heard that General Bayard, our division commander, was mortally wounded. Soon after word came that cavalry was needed. Two regiments of the enemy were running, it was said, and the Harris Light Cavalry was wanted to follow them up. Off dashed our men in close column, at full gallop, to the place designated, the surgeon and myself going to the hospital to prepare for our wounded. As we started, the road over which the regiment had just passed, and directly in front of us, was torn up by a solid shot. Whose earnest prayers were heard that day, and the Harris Light Cavalry saved from almost a massacre? The order for cavalry had to pass through three different hands before it reached us, and by the time our men arrived at the spot it was discovered that the enemy's retreat was only a feint, and that batteries were so arranged as to place the party who should follow them between two fires. Our regiment approached near enough to the trap, and were exposed to a sufficiently hot fire, for a few minutes, to be satisfied that if they had charged, as was intended, but few would have returned.

" At the hospital we found poor Bayard. Of all the ghastly wounds I saw that day his was the most awful. It needed but a glance to see, as he calmly stated to those who visited him, " that his days on earth were numbered." If his wound had been a mere scratch, he could not have been more cool, quiet, and collected. He talked calmly of his death as of a settled thing, and only inquired particularly how much time he had left on earth. He was told, 'perhaps forty-eight hours.' He did not live twenty-four. My heart sank within me as he gave me his hand in farewell, and I almost murmured, 'Why are the best taken?' The large house to which the wounded were brought was now filled with mutilated and dying men. Cries and groans resounded from every apartment. Ghastly and bloody wounds met the eye in every direction. Some had their eyes shot out; the tongues of some were swollen out of their mouths; some had their bodies shot through; others were torn and mangled by shell and solid shot, and all were crowded wherever there was any space. The surgeons were hacking off limbs and arms by the dozen. The odor of blood was oppressive. One man called me to him, thinking I was a surgeon, and said that one of his wounds had been dressed, but he found that he had another, which was bleeding rapidly. Another poor fellow held up his arm to me, with a great bulging hole in it, and asked with an expression of pain and anxiety that I could scarcely endure, whether I thought he would have to lose it? Such is the horrid reality of war behind the painted scenes of honor, glory, and romance. However cold an ear the poor fellows may have turned to the story of the Cross when in health, as a general thing they were ready enough now to listen to the offers of mercy. One wounded boy had his leg taken off just as he was entering the hospital, which building was under fire all day, and was repeatedly struck. The scene from the windows of the hospital was truly splendid as night came on. Innumerable camp-fires gleamed from the hillsides, and occasionally the darkness was lighted up by the flash of cannon. But weariness, and the knowledge that our own regiment might be engaged the next day, caused me to seek a place of rest. The medical department of our brigade had been rendered small by the absence of some of its members, and it might be that our duties on the morrow would be very arduous. The ground outside the hospital was so tramped up, muddy, and filled with horses, that it was impossible to sleep there. But there was a stone alley-way under the hospital, filled with tobacco in the leaf, part of it lying on the ground, and part drying overhead. One end of this place was already filled with wounded men, but the surgeon in charge said that the other would not be occupied before morning, and that I had better stay there. As a light came I saw something white lying near the wall. I first thought it was a dog, and going up, I stirred the object with my foot. On looking closer, I found that it was a ghastly pile of arms and legs from the amputating-room. But I had seen so much of blood and horror during the day that I had grown callous. I quietly spread my blanket within ten feet of the bloody heap, and listened sadly to the shrieks and groans from the hospital above till I fell asleep. The reopening of the battle on Sunday morning awoke me, and as I was rolling up my blankets, a shell bursting near warned me to hasten. I joined the regiment, and with it recrossed the river. We have since been doing picket duty on the Rappahannock.

E. P. ROE AS CHAPLAIN, AGE 26.

" Many a careless, light-hearted soldier wore an anxious, troubled look that day, as we stood facing the rebel batteries, and many a loud-mouthed, coarse, swearing fellow was quiet and pale. But I saw no flinching or skulking. You at the North, who cosily read about battles in an arm-chair, know little of a man's sensations who stands in front of the enemy's guns. He hears shot and shell scream and explode over and around him. Before him arises the sulphurous smoke of the conflict. From out of that obscurity he knows that at any moment some swift messenger of death may be speeding on its way to his heart. He thinks of unfinished plans, of bright prospects and hopes for the future. His home, its beloved inmates, and the forms and features of those friends that hold the chief places within his soul rise up before him, and he knows that at any moment he may be snatched from all these, and lie a mangled, bleeding corpse upon the ground. And then come graver and still more solemn thoughts of the shadowy world beyond, and 'conscience, which makes cowards of us all,' awakes. In the mad excitement and tumult of a charge, everything is forgotten. When patiently standing under fire, everything is remembered, and this, of all that the soldier has to do and endure, is the most difficult and dreaded."

An occasional amusing incident would occur,

however, to relieve the gloom of these tragic times. I remember hearing my brother tell of one that took place while crossing a narrow pontoon bridge. A mule, ridden by a contraband, and having a number of kettles strung on one side of the saddle and on the other some chickens that had been captured from henroosts along the march, suddenly became stubborn when about half-way across the bridge, and resisted all efforts on the part of his rider to make him move on. He was blocking the way for the whole troop. An officer, seeing the situation, shouted the order: "Charge mule!" Instantly half a dozen men rode up and with the points of their sabres convinced the animal of the necessity for a speedy advance. He started off at a dead run, scattering the rattling kettles and squawking hens by the wayside, the poor contraband holding on with arms clasped around the mule's neck, while the troopers followed in wild pursuit, amid shouts and laughter.

CHAPTER III

A WINTER CAMP

THE following letters were written from the winter quarters of the regiment on the Rappahannock, and explain themselves.

"In this letter I merely propose to give some glimpses of camp life. When the army lay quiet for two or three weeks after the battle of Fredericksburg, we began to think of winter quarters; so one fine morning our whole division started out in search of a desirable locality. In some respects it was a rather novel expedition. We were seeking a place that would probably be our home for months; and I assure you, as we marched along, that unknown spot of ground became to us an object of no small anxiety and interest. Those officers who had designs on Washington, rather than Richmond, hoped it would be near the steamboat landing on the Potomac. Many wishes were expressed that wood would be plenty and convenient; for winter quarters without wood is an impossibility. Speculations were indulged in regard to the locality and soil, whether it would be a dry, sheltered little valley, or a bleak cornfield capable of all degrees of mud. The place of encampment selected for our regiment was apparently the latter. I must say that many of us were not very enthusiastic about the position, and we could not feel indifferent, for our comfort and perhaps health depended on the suitableness of the place.

"Imagine yourself, my reader, riding into a large, bleak, hilly cornfield, the stalks still standing, with your whole personal property in this region of the world strapped behind you on the saddle, your horse sinking at every step fetlock deep in the soft, spongy soil, and being coolly told to make yourself comfortable here for the winter. Probably you would feel as we suppose the Israelites did when required to make bricks without straw. But necessity and experience have taught the soldier many lessons, and he knows well how to make the best of everything. In a few minutes the long picket lines are uncoiled and stretched from post to post inserted for the purpose. To these the horses are tied and then unsaddled. The little shelter tents range themselves, as if by magic, in long rows between them, and within a half-hour or so the place begins to assume the appearance of a well laid out encampment.

"But this is merely temporary, and the building

of regular winter quarters is next in order. The
size and character of the huts being left to the
fancy and ingenuity of each individual, there is,
with much apparent sameness, a great deal of
diversity and originality to be observed. The
most simple is merely a 'dug-out,' as it is termed.
A hole is dug six or seven feet square, and from
two to four feet deep, and over this is placed the
tent. The floor and sides are lined with boards if
they are to be had, otherwise round poles and rails
answer the purpose. Opening into this 'dug-
out' is a small trench two or three feet long, wide
at its mouth, and narrowing towards the end
farthest from the tent. Across this trench are
laid any old pieces of iron that can be found, and
upon them is placed earth so as to exclude the air
entirely except at a small aperture at the farther
end, around which is built a sod chimney; and
your winter quarters are complete. Thus you
may have in your tent all the warmth and cheer-
fulness of an open fire.

"Myself and servant alone built one of these in
an afternoon, and I spent in it some of the coldest
weather we have had this winter very comfortably.
The 'dug-out' principle enters into the construction of nearly all our little cabins; and, like the
foxes, we have holes, and literally live in the
'caves and dens of the earth.' The officers gen-

erally build their quarters in the side of a bank, and have them logged up nicely, and they are very comfortable except in a long storm. Sometimes our frail canvas covering sways terribly in the wintry blasts, and I have often laid down to sleep more than half expecting to find my house gone when I awoke. Still our little holes in the ground are a hundredfold better than no shelter at all, and far preferable to those in which the soldier 'sleeps the sleep that knows no waking.' Some of the men who have the faculty of making anything and everything with an axe put up quite large substantial log shanties, with two or three tiers of berths, as in a steamboat. Some have quite a neat, homelike appearance, and are furnished with fanciful little tables and shelves according to the tastes and wants of the occupants. Others are dismal and dirty in the extreme, and are mere dens. Nothing shows the character of the men more thoroughly than the little huts they inhabit. A few are too indolent to build themselves anything, and are still living in their shelter tents. But over the heads of us all is merely a canvas roof, which will often leak, and it is a very common thing to see puddles of water, or a muddy floor, in our winter quarters.

" Still those who are well live in the main a very comfortable life. The abundance of pure

air and exercise makes us strong and vigorous.
It does not always storm. We have many days
that are warm and sunny, and then give me camp
life in preference to any other. The soldiers sit
and lounge around their cabin doors in motley
groups, reading (if they have anything to read),
smoking, and gossiping, for a camp is a little
miniature city, with its daily budget of news and
sensations, its streets, squares, and centers, and
also many of its nuisances. For the roar of New
York we have a drowsy, diminutive hum, frequently broken rudely by a loud laugh or command, the clangor of weapons, and sometimes, I
am sorry to say, by loud oaths. Instead of musical chimes from Trinity and her sister steeples, the
silvery notes of the bugles proclaim the hours and
duties of the day. Our lights glimmer and flicker
out upon the night like long rows of glowworms
rather than Broadway lamps; and instead of the
heavy tramp of police armed with star and club,
the night-long rattle of sabres shows that the
guards and sentinels are on their posts of duty.
Sometimes there will be a heavy fall of snow during the night, and then the tents and cabins look
like huge snow-banks, and the poor horses shiver
all the more under the cold white blankets so
summarily furnished, the only ones they ever get.
These suffer more than the men, for in the main

they can have no shelter, and often have to do hard work on short rations. Their gaunt appearance and the number of their dead tells its own story. Our colonel remarked one day that he hoped the mud would get so soft and deep that the horses would sink in sufficiently to enable them to stand upright.

"The greatest hardship of a soldier's life in winter is picket duty. For instance, our whole brigade, recently assigned to Colonel Kilpatrick, left their comfortable quarters a few mornings ago, and went out on picket duty for ten days. A cold, wet snow filled the air and clung to and dampened everything. It settled on one's hair and neck, melted, and ran down his back, producing a general feeling of discomfort. As the men formed preparatory to marching, their uniforms of blue rapidly changed to white, and as they filed off in the dim morning light they presented a shadowy, ghost-like appearance. When you realize what it is to march eighteen or twenty miles in such a storm over horrible roads, and then form a cordon of pickets twenty miles long in a wild, desolate country, you have some idea of the not unusual experience of a soldier.

"When he reaches his destination, it is not a disagreeable journey over, and comfortable quarters in which to dry and refresh himself. All his conditions of comfort are carried on his person, or strapped to his saddle, and he is thankful even for the shelter of a pine wood. Immediately on arrival, without time for rest, a large detachment must form the picket line, and stand ever on the alert from two to four hours at a time, be it day or night. It should not be forgotten, during these long winter evenings when the stormy wind sweeps and howls around your comfortable dwellings, that among the wild woods and hills of Virginia, or on the plains of the far West, the patient sentinel walks his desolate beat, or sits like an equestrian statue on his horse, thus forming with his own chilled and weary frame a living breastwork and defence for your homes. Pray for him, that during these long, lonely hours of hardship and danger our merciful God may excite within his mind thoughts of that better life and happier world where the weary are at rest — where even the names of enemy and war are forgotten."

"The regiment referred to is the Ninth New York Cavalry. Their chaplain is not with them at present. My offer to preach for them on the Sabbath was readily accepted, and though at the time of service it was cold and even raining slightly, a large congregation turned out and remained patiently throughout the service. One of their officers remarked afterwards that he had not had the pleasure of attending anything of the kind before for five months.

"If Christians North, who have piles of reading matter lying idly about their houses, could see how eagerly those men pressed forward to get the few tracts I offered, they would suffer it to remain thus useless no longer. Our soldiers seem to be hungry and almost starving for the want of mental and moral nourishment.

"I often feel it my duty to be somewhat officious, and to offer my service outside of my regiment sometimes, for even such as I can give is better than nothing, which would be their lot if some did not go forward. I think Christians should be aggressive in their character, and seek opportunities to extend the dominion of their King. There are too many professors who are like a certain chaplain, concerning whom I heard an officer remark "that he was a good, inoffensive man, and never disturbed the devil nor any one else in the camp." A prayer-meeting was appointed on Monday evening, but on the morning of that day the regiment received marching orders and departed for parts unknown.

"One of the most remarkable conversions in our regiment is that of a quartermaster's sergeant. The man, although around the camp attending to his duties, is in a critical state of health, bleeding almost daily at the lungs. When but a mere boy he ran away from home because punished severely by his father for some fault, and was not heard from for over two years, during which time he suffered many hardships in the West. Not long after his discovery his father died and left a mother and a sister dependent upon him for support. This responsibility he nobly undertook, and worked hard, early and late, and denied himself everything to give them the comforts of life. Still, he was noted for his fiery and ungovernable spirit, which often got him into trouble. At an early age he went to sea and visited nearly all parts of the world. He engaged extensively in smuggling, which occupation he followed both in English and Spanish waters. He returned home from this roving, reckless life but a short time before the war broke out, and was among the first to enlist. During the past summer he has often been in circumstances of the greatest peril, but escaped unharmed. Once, in the confusion of battle, he found himself directly in front of a battery loaded with grape and canister. For some reason or other his horse would not move but stood stock still, and thus he had to wait for the terrible discharge which soon came. He said it seemed as if a perfect torrent of iron hail rushed by and all around him, and that his only thought was that his time had come now, and that the devil had got him then surely. By a miracle, as it seemed to him, he escaped unharmed, and was enabled to get out of range. Many and many a time he had heard the bullets hiss by his ears, and the shrill screams of shell overhead, but they raised in his mind no thoughts of God or repentance.

"As I described in a former letter, a prayer-meeting was started in the camp, and held in the quarters of the new recruits. He heard the singing, and passing by the next day remarked to a new recruit that 'they seemed happy down there last night — guessed they must have had some whiskey.' The person addressed happened to be one of the three Christian men who first started the prayer-meeting, and he explained to the sergeant the somewhat different source and occasion of their happiness. The sergeant promised to attend that evening, which he did, and the 'still small voice' of the Spirit spoke to him louder than the thunders of the battlefield.

"An evening or two after that I noticed him among those who had come to the chaplain's tent to be conversed with on the subject of religion. I was struck by the contented, happy expression of his face. He told me that he had gone from that prayer-meeting to his tent, and commenced read-

ing a Testament. His tent-mate came along, and
he immediately put out his light and hid his
book. When he was alone again he knelt and
prayed for the first time in his life, and afterwards, he said, 'he felt so happy he could not
sleep.'

"The next day, while about his work, something
vexed him, and he swore, before he thought, as
usual. He said 'it grieved him so that he sat
down and cried.' Though, as it were, alone in
the world and bereft by death of almost every
friend he loved, and now seemingly suffering from
an incurable disease, he is a happy Christian
man.

"In our meetings he has to be constantly on his
guard against over-excitement, since it would cause
him to bleed at his lungs, but the expression of his
face, as he sits quietly in one corner or beside the
fire, shows how intense and keen is his enjoyment
of that which he is forbidden to take part in actively.
At first his change of life caused a good deal of
remark and some merriment in his company. He
would be asked 'when he was going up to
heaven.' When he commenced his evening devotions there was at first a good deal of jesting.
'The quartermaster is going to pray' would be
called out, and remarks of a similar nature. They
soon saw that he was sincere and respected him,

and 'now,' he says, 'he can hear a pin drop while he is at prayer.'

"This is one of many of the interesting cases of conversion in our regiment. The chief feature of this work, however, seems to be the renewal of backsliders in their allegiance to God. But time will not permit me to write more at present."

"How often when a boy I have shuddered at Indian atrocities. With what morbid pleasure I have searched through the early records of colonial history for details of horror, fatal surprise, and midnight massacre. How I have watched in imagination, with suspended breath, the wary, noiseless approach of the painted savages, till with one wide-ringing war-whoop they rushed upon their unconscious victims, destined now to either death or captivity. The dangers and terrors of open battle seemed nothing to this constant dread of an unseen treacherous foe. I little thought that it would one day be my fortune to live under very similar circumstances, for life in Virginia now is not so very different from that of our forefathers a century or more ago. Pioneers in this wilderness of despotism and treason, we are exposed to dangers and hardships not much inferior to theirs. Ever near us we know there is a great army watching with sleepless vigilance, and, like a wild beast crouching for its leap, it is ready to take advantage of the slightest mistake or show of weakness on our part. It is very strange, truly, when one comes to realize it, this living for years within a few miles of thousands who would take your life in a moment if they got a chance.

" The forests and country around us swarm with guerillas. In place of some savage Indian chief, the terror of the whole border, the frontiers of our army are infested by the ubiquitous Mosby. The capture of a sutler's train near Fairfax and a raid upon an outpost on the Rappahannock occurring at the same time are both ascribed to Mosby in person by the soldiers. If a picket hears a distant gallop in the night upon one flank of the army, and a sudden shot startles the air upon the other flank, Mosby is invariably the author of both alarms. No wonder the poor contrabands say ' Mosby mus' be like de debbel and go all ober to oncst.' He was once captured by our regiment while bearing dispatches and afterwards exchanged. After he was taken he tried to escape by running his horse, but one of our men sent a bullet whistling so near his head that it produced a sober second thought, and he, from that time, followed quietly. But he was not so famous then, and had not so many trained associates like-minded with himself. Now they follow a marching column like hungry sharks about a ship, and woe be to the man that lags behind or strays from the main body.

" This evil has one great advantage, however, and that is the almost entire suppression of straggling. Mosby and his companions have done more to abolish this disgraceful custom in our army than all the orders and edicts from the War Department and Major Generals down. A year or more ago, I saw bodies of men marching in a way that reminded one of a comet, the head of the regiment being the nucleus, the density decreasing rapidly as you went toward the rear, and finally a straggling raft of men scattered over two or three miles of territory constituting the tail. Now you will find a column moving trimly and compactly, and the rear files often looking suspiciously over their shoulders among the dark pines through which they are passing, for sometimes, especially at nights, shots are fired into the rear.

" There are very few in the cavalry that have not had narrow escapes, for our position on the front and flanks of the army always brings us next to Mosby. Just before we crossed the Rappahannock the last time, our division commissary, Lieutenant Hedges, was returning to his quarters from a short ride to another part of the army, when he was hailed and ordered to surrender. ' Never,' he

replied, at the same time striking spurs to his
horse and leaning down upon him. He succeeded
in escaping, but not before the guerilla, or as it is
affirmed, Mosby in person, put a ball through
his body. For some days he was not expected to
live, but is now recovering slowly. I have had
two or three narrow escapes myself where it
almost seemed that Providence interfered to save
my life. Once, when our regiment was doing
picket duty at a distant outpost, I rode down to
General Kilpatrick's headquarters on some business. As I was starting to return in the dusk of
the evening, the general came out and asked me
to stay with him that night. I replied that with
his permission I would come again in the morning,
and that I would rather be with my regiment at
night; but as he insisted upon it, I stayed. The
next morning, a little after daylight, one of our
men was shot dead and robbed upon the road that I
would have taken. A woman living near said that
two bushwhackers had spent the night upon the
road with the avowed intention of murdering and
robbing the first man that went by. As no one
passed that way during the early part of the night,
they went into a house and slept till morning, and
again were on the road in time to meet poor
Francher of Company B, who had been after his
pay. They took this, for his pocket was found

turned inside out. It was my sad duty to bury him the next day, and as we lowered him into his lonely grave, I could not help asking myself, Why am I not in his place?

" Once again, last November, while on the march, Lieutenant Whitaker and myself were about to pass over a road between our wagon train and General Kilpatrick's headquarters, when a little incident detained us about fifteen minutes. As we were going by the house of quite a noted secessionist, some of our boys began to make free in his cabbage garden and poultry yard, and a scuffle ensued between the old citizen, his wife and daughter, and the soldiers. An infantry colonel who was at the house came violently out, and instead of quietly showing his rank and firmly ordering the men away, commenced cutting them with his sword, and made some quite serious wounds. It was with great difficulty that we prevented our men from killing him on the spot. But as the colonel outranked us, we could do nothing with him, and so passed on, but before we got fairly started upon the road again we met a man running, breathless, with his hat off, who said that he had just escaped from the guerillas. Lieutenant Newton of the First Vermont Cavalry was passing over the road with several men, when fifteen rebels sprang out upon him, killed one, took two prisoners, and the rest saved themselves only by rapid flight. If we had not been detained, we would have arrived at the same spot a few minutes earlier and received their concentrated fire.

"At times they have captured our mail, and afterwards they have taunted us by shouting out the contents of our letters to our pickets across the Rappahannock. One very dark night they slipped into the quarters of one of our officers while he was on picket, shot his colored servant, and carried him off to Richmond. Thus vigilance is a cardinal virtue in this, as well as in the Christian warfare. But we never suffered as much on the south as on the north side of the Rappahannock. The country between the two rivers is now thoroughly occupied by our troops, and our picket lines so close and well posted as to render it almost impossible for the rebels to indulge themselves this winter in many murdering and horse-stealing expeditions."

CHAPTER IV

MARRIAGE — THE RAID TOWARD RICHMOND

IN November, 1863, Edward received a month's leave of absence from his regiment, and during this time was married to Miss Anna Sands. The ceremony was performed by the venerable Dr. Adams in Madison Square church, and was followed by a large reception at the bride's home in Seventeenth Street, New York. Leaving his bride there when the furlough was over, my brother returned to his regiment.

In this letter, written just after reaching camp, he dwells upon some of the contrasts of army life.

"After a long absence I experienced a decided thrill of pleasure on finding myself once more among the white tents and familiar scenes of the camp, for there is something very fascinating about army life, notwithstanding its hardship and exposure. Very pleasant, too, was the hearty welcome I received, and numberless great brown hands, reeking with moisture and pork grease from the meal they were superintending, gave me a grip that made my joints snap again. Still I much preferred it to your fashionable Northern two-fingered touch. It had a language whose meaning I liked. It showed I had the first requisite for doing good amongst them — their confidence and affection. I found only a part, though a large part, of my regiment at·this place, which is a dis-mounted cavalry camp, containing the fragments of twenty or thirty regiments. Men whose horses have given out or been killed at the front come here and remain till they are again mounted and equipped, when they rejoin their commands. Our stay here will probably be brief, for we are ordered to the front as soon as possible.

" One Saturday morning the monotony of camp life was decidedly broken. The day had been warm, and for a time the hum of camp activity had subsided almost into silence. The orderlies went to and fro as usual, but their horses had a listless, indolent canter, characteristic of all exer-tion at such a time. But as the day declined there were marks of unusual bustle at headquarters. A ball was to be given that evening by the com-manding officer. All officers present of our regi-ment were invited. As far as I could learn, music, dancing, and drinking were to be the staple amuse-ments of the evening. Not caring to participate in the two latter, and as I could enjoy the first in my tent, I expected to remain very quietly at my quarters. At dusk the revelry commenced. At nine o'clock a carriage drove up to our quarters. It contained Captain Downing of our regiment, who had just come in from the front, bringing with him the dead body of one of our officers who had been drowned while bathing. This was sad news indeed, for Lieutenant Stewart was a good soldier and very popular. The captain wished to see the officer in command of our detachment. I went up to the headquarters to assist in finding him. All was gayety and frolic there. It was truly a beautiful scene. The trees were hung with Chinese lanterns of many colors. The guards paced backward and forward on the spacious lawn, their arms glittering in the moonlight, which glimmered through the grand old trees. In the distance the Potomac lay like a silver lake, with here and there a white sail upon its bosom. Over the green turf gayly dressed ladies and officers in rich uniform were tripping some light measure, while the clinking of glasses showed that the wine was passing freely. No one could help enjoying the music from the full military band.

" Having noted the picturesque beauty of the scene, and moralized to myself awhile unnoticed among the throng, I thought I would step over to the hospital and see how the sick boys were enjoying the revel. It was not over fifty yards from the music-stand. Though it might be pleasure to others, it was death to them. One poor fellow, far gone with the typhoid fever, and excited by the music and noise, was talking to himself in wild delirium. He has since died. All were restless and sleepless. I said a few quieting words, and was about leaving when a man asked me if I would not offer a prayer. "I am not a Christian man," he remarked, "but I would like to hear a prayer to-night." Of course I complied, and soon the words of supplication were mingling with the gay notes of the quickstep. I have seen the man since several times, and have good reason to believe that he has become a sincere, earnest Christian. The contrast in his two modes of life will be most marked. He told me that when at home he would often take his wife to church, and then ride on further and trade horses during the service, and call for his wife on his return. As may be imagined, army life had not improved his morals. Still the influence of his Christian wife followed him, and during his days of sickness came back in tenfold power, and the kindly Spirit of our merciful Father, ever-striving, led him to the Saviour.

"After leaving the hospital I met the sergeant of the guard, and found him arming a body of men.

" We are going to have trouble to-night," he said
to me. The camp below was in a ferment. There
were many there who loved whisky as well as the
more privileged at headquarters. At first the
rioters (who were mainly from a regiment of regu-
lars) threatened to appropriate the officers' stores
and break up the ball. But hardly daring to do that,
they turned their attention to a sutler's tent and
eating-house. They soon demolished his establishment and set fire to his premises. They here
obtained the much desired whisky, and excited by
liquor, they boldly began preparations to attack
another sutler who was unpopular. The riot was
now getting formidable. From my tent I could
overlook the whole camp and scenes at headquarters. Meantime our regiment was arming
and procuring ammunition. Fifty of our men were
already acting as guards. They formed and received their cartridges in front of our tents, thus
drawing attention to the headquarters of our detachment, which I thought at one time would pro-
voke an attack upon us. I dreaded this, for one
of our officers had left his wife in my charge at the
commencement of the disturbance. Our men then
marched to headquarters, fearing the first attack
would be there. For a few moments all was still
throughout the camp. Then there were signals in
all directions. In a few moments more the mules

were stampeded from the corrall. They then pro-
ceeded to attack the sutler's tent just below us.
Here the guards fired upon them, which caused
them to retreat to the burning sutler's tent in the
middle of the camp. Then I could see our men
coming down from the headquarters on a full run.
Wheeling at a certain point, they charged without
a moment's hesitation. For a short time shots
were fired in rapid succession, when the rioters
broke and ran. The ball was arrested. The order
was given, ' Every officer to his post.' The ladies,
pale and frightened, were huddled together, asking
anxious questions. Many of the officers might
be seen in their ball-dress walking and riding
through the camp with sword and pistol driving
the men into their tents. Such volleys of horrible
oaths as were heard in every direction I hope may
never shock my ears again. Officers cursed the
men, and the men cursed the officers. For a time
things looked rather serious. Meanwhile our boys
stood grim and expectant, ready to quell any show
of resistance. In a few minutes the whole camp
was under arms, but the ringleaders having been
caught, quiet was eventually restored. My heart
ached for the young wife who saw the exposure of
her husband and felt her own danger, and who was
compelled to listen to the awful profanity of the
hour. I will say, for the benefit of all concerned,

that there was nothing of a political nature in the outbreak. Whatever may be the soldiers' vices, they have not yet sunk so far as to sympathize with Northern 'copperheads.' The cause, as far as I could learn, was the unpopularity of the sutlers, jealousy of our regiment because the guard of honor for the evening was chosen from it, and a desire for whisky, for which a certain class will do and dare anything. After quiet was restored the dancing, music, and drinking were resumed as though nothing had happened. Meanwhile, on one side the poor fellows in the hospital tossed and moaned and raved in their restlessness and delirium, and on the other lay the two rioters stiff and stark upon the ground, their souls rudely thrust out into the unknown amidst riot and intoxication, soon to be sobered but too well by their abrupt plunge into the dusk waters of death. Life presents to the close observer peculiar phases and contrasts at all times, but it seems that in the events of this evening there was a strange mingling of life and death, pleasure and pain. Yet in the sick and repentant soldier God was at least fashioning one soul from out this moral and social chaos for the perfect symmetry of heaven. I had hoped that after the night's uproar we should have a quiet Sabbath, but was disappointed in this, for orders came in the morning to arm, mount, and equip every available man and send them all to the front. And so throughout the day the clangor of arms, the trampling of men and horses, and the words of command, made the quiet peacefulness of a Northern Sabbath a thing scarcely to be imagined."

Late in February, 1864, Edward joined General Kilpatrick in his famous raid towards Richmond. He wrote a brief account of this, which was published in *Lippincott's Magazine*.

"In the dusk of Sunday evening four thousand men were masked in the woods on the banks of the Rapidan. Our scouts opened the way by wading the stream and pouncing upon the unsuspecting picket of twenty Confederates opposite. Then away we went across a cold, rapid river, marching all that night through the dim woods and openings in a country that was emphatically the enemy's. Lee's entire army was on our right, the main Confederate cavalry force on our left. The strength of our column and its objective point could not remain long unknown.

"In some unimportant ways I acted as aid for Kilpatrick. A few hundred yards in advance of the main body rode a vanguard of two hundred men thrown forward to warn us should we strike any considerable number of the enemy's cavalry.

5

As is ever the case, the horses of a small force will walk away from a much larger body, and it was necessary from time to time to send word to the vanguard, ordering it to 'slow up.' This order was occasionally intrusted to me. I was to gallop over the interval between the two columns, then draw up by the roadside and sit motionless on my horse till the general with his staff came up. The slightest irregularity of action would bring a shot from our own men, while the prospect of an interview with the Johnnies while thus isolated was always good. I saw one of our officers shot that night. He had ridden carelessly into the woods, and rode out again just before the head of the column, without instantly accounting for himself. As it was of vital importance to keep the movement secret as long as possible, the poor fellow was silenced in sad error as to his identity.

"On we rode, night and day, with the briefest possible halts. At one point we nearly captured a railroad train, and might easily have succeeded had not the station and warehouses been in flames. As it was, the train approached us closely, then backed, the shrieking engine giving the impression of being startled to the last degree.

"On a dreary, drizzling, foggy day we passed a milestone on which was lettered, 'Four miles to Richmond.' It was still 'on to Richmond' with us for what seemed a long way farther, and then came a considerable period of hesitancy, in which the command was drawn up for the final dash. The enemy shelled a field near us vigorously, but fortunately, or unfortunately, the fog was so dense that neither party could make accurate observations or do much execution.

"For reasons that have passed into history, the attack was not made. We withdrew six miles from the city and went into camp.

"I had scarcely begun to enjoy much-needed rest before the Confederates came up in the darkness and shelled us out of such quarters as we had found. We had to leave our boiling coffee behind us — one of the greatest hardships I have ever known. Then followed a long night ride down the Peninsula, in driving sleet and rain.

"The next morning the sun broke out gloriously, warming and drying our chilled, wet forms. Nearly all that day we maintained a line of battle confronting the pursuing enemy. One brigade would take a defensive position, while the other would march about five miles to a commanding point, where it in turn would form a line. The first brigade would then give way, pass through the second, and take position well to the rear. Thus, although retreating, we were always ready to fight. At one point the enemy pressed us closely, and I saw a magnificent cavalry charge down a gentle descent in the road.   Every sabre seemed tipped with fire in the brilliant sunshine.

" In the afternoon it became evident that there was a body of troops before us.   Who or what they were was at first unknown, and for a time the impression prevailed that we would have to cut our way through by a headlong charge.   We soon learned, however, that the force was a brigade of colored infantry, sent up to cover our retreat.   It was the first time we had seen negro troops, but as the long line of glistening bayonets and light-blue uniforms came into view, prejudices, if any there were, vanished at once, and a cheer from the begrimed troopers rang down our line, waking the echoes.   It was a pleasant thing to march past that array of faces, friendly though black, and know we were safe.   They represented the F. F. V.'s of Old Virginia we then wished to see.   On the last day of the march my horse gave out, compelling me to walk and lead him.

" On the day after our arrival at Yorktown Kilpatrick gave me despatches for the authorities at Washington.   President Lincoln, learning that I had just returned from the raid, sent for me, and I had a memorable interview with him alone in his private room.   He expressed profound solicitude for Colonel Dahlgren and his party. They had been detached from the main force, and I could give no information concerning them. We eventually learned of the death of that heroic young officer, Colonel Dahlgren."

CHAPTER V

HAMPTON HOSPITAL

IN March, 1864, Edward began his duties as chaplain of Hampton Hospital, having been appointed to this position before the raid described in the preceding chapter was undertaken. Mrs. Roe joined him at Washington and they went to Hampton together. A tribute is here due the brave young wife, who, leaving a home of luxury, accepted without a word of regret the privations of hospital life and was untiring in her devotion to the sick and wounded. The letters which follow show what that life was during the last two years of the war. The first is an appeal for books for the sick soldiers made through *The Evangelist*, and is preceded by a note of explanation from the editors of that paper.

"We have received the following letter from the esteemed and efficient chaplain of the Hampton Hospital, Virginia, Rev. Mr. Roe, who, as it will be seen, is desirous of securing a well-selected soldiers' library for the use of the hospital. Many of our readers formed an agreeable acquaintance

with Mr. Roe, through his correspondence with
The Evangelist while chaplain of the Harris Light
Cavalry; and we would refer all others for an
estimate of the man, as also of the nature and extent of his duties in his new position, to an interesting paper in the August number of *Harper's
Magazine*, on the Chesapeake and Hampton Hospitals.   We shall take pleasure in aiding this
praiseworthy object in every way in our power,
and we trust that the money required for the purchase of these books will be speedily contributed.

'U. S. GENERAL HOSPITAL, FORTRESS MONROE, VA.
July 27, 1864.

'READERS OF THE EVANGELIST: — Pardon me
if I say a few plain words in preface to a request.
I wish to appeal to a quality that I hope is univer-
sal — gratitude.   That the North is grateful for the
self-sacrifice of its soldiers is well proved by its
noble charities in their behalf.   But, my Northern
friends, you who dwell securely in beautiful and
healthful homes, can you not give a little more for
those who are giving all for you?

'The U. S. General Hospital at Hampton, Va., is
very large this summer.   The average is two thousand five hundred patients, and we often have three
thousand.   Accommodations are in process of construction for still larger numbers.   This is now the

nearest permanent hospital to General Grant's army. Almost daily transports from the front leave at our wharf sick and mutilated men by hundreds, and we in turn send those North who are able to bear further transportation. Thus our wards become mainly filled with what are termed the "worst cases" — men with whom the struggle for life will be long and doubtful. I could take you through our wards, and show you long rows of men with thigh amputations, fractured thighs; men who have lost arms, hands, and both their feet; and in short, men with great gaping, ghastly wounds in every part of the body. With such injuries nothing will sustain but cheerful courage; despondency is almost always fatal. The only true basis of such courage is God's religion, but to this all-important condition much can be added that is most excellent. But could you ask for more than these men have done and suffered? I think they have done their part. Yours is not so hard, but it is important. In your abundant provisions for their suffering bodies, do not forget rations for their minds. There are hundreds in this hospital who must lie upon their beds, weeks, and even months, before they can even hope to hobble out into the world again with crutch and cane. How shall they spend these long, hot, weary days? Give them cheerful, entertaining, instructive books, and the question is about solved. Who can calculate the value of a brave, cheerful book? It stimulates and strengthens the mind, which reacts upon the weakened body, and the man is at once made stronger, wiser, and better. I felt that first of all I ought to have a religious library, and through some effort, and the kindness of friends, have obtained a very fair collection. But cheerful, light, entertaining books are few and far between, while there is almost an entire dearth of histories, travels, etc. I find that sick soldiers, even the best of them, are like good people North, they do not like religious reading all the time. The works of Irving, John S. C. Abbott, Dickens, Cooper, Scott, and T. S. Arthur, would be invaluable from both a sanitary and a moral point of view, for they would remove the parent of all evils— idleness. Poetry also is very much asked for. My simple request, therefore, is that out of gratitude to the brave suffering men who throng the wards of Hampton Hospital, you would send them good cheerful books. I have an excellent librarian, and I promise that they shall be carefully looked after and preserved. Among the thousands who have been here and gone away, I have scarcely lost a book.

'Messrs. Harpers, and Appletons, and other prominent city publishers, have generously offered me their books at half price for hospital purposes. All contributions in money sent to me, or to the offices of the New York *Evangelist*, *The Observer*, and the Brooklyn *Daily Union*, will be promptly and judiciously laid out for such books as are needed. All contributions in books sent to the above-named places will be forwarded to the hospital in my care.'"

Some years after the war was over, my brother took a trip to Fortress Monroe and visited the scenes of his former labors. I quote from a letter telling of the result of his appeal for a soldier's library and of the subsequent use that was made of the books.

"We entered the fort, presented our letter to General Barry, in command, who received us with the utmost courtesy. The band discoursed delightful music. We examined the mitrailleuse, of which the world has heard so much of late. One of the most interesting points to me was the Post Library. Here among many others I found all the books that once formed our hospital library. Loyal Northern friends, who were ever caring for the soldier's well-being, enabled me to gather and purchase about three thousand volumes. I know that it will be gratifying to them to learn that their gifts, so far from being lost or destroyed, are all here in excellent order, and still doing the work for which they were designed. When a book becomes badly worn it is sent away and rebound. The private soldiers, of which there are several hundred, as well as the officers, have free access to them. I was told by the soldier in charge that between two and three hundred of these books were taken out and read monthly. Under General Barry's careful supervision they will be in use for years to come. He evidently regards his men as something more than machines."

It was inevitable that my brother should witness many sad partings during those long years of conflict, and the strain upon his sympathies was very great, as may be seen from the letters that follow.

" Among the painful and tragic events that occurred in our hospital at Fortress Monroe, there was one wherein heaven and earth were strangely mingled. The arm of a strong, powerful man had been amputated at the shoulder joint. He was full of vitality and made a long but vain struggle for life. Day after day, and week after week, he lay, scarcely daring to move, lest the artery should break and his life blood ebb away. But ever at his side (it seemed to me that she almost never left him) sat his true, patient wife. Strange and incongruous did her slight and graceful form, her pale, beautiful face appear in that place of wounds and death. The rough soldiers were never rough or profane in her presence, and their kindly sympathy often touched me. For long weeks the scale turned for neither life nor death, but at last the sharp agony of hope and fear ended in the dull pain of despair. He must die. The artery broke and bled again and again, and skill would soon be of no avail. Some time previous to this, a message had come to the poor wife that her mother was dying, and she was requested to return home immediately.

"'No,' she said, 'my mother is among friends; my husband is alone; I must stay with him.'

"Late one night, when the certainty of death was apparent, they sent for me, and we three had a long, calm talk in the dim, crowded ward. The brave, true soldier did not regret that he had entered his country's service, though it cost him so dearly, but he spoke a few words in regard to those who caused the war that must ever hang upon them like millstones. Turning to his young wife with an affection beautiful to look upon, he said: —

"'Mary, you have prepared me to die, now you must go home and do the same for your poor mother.'

"These brief words revealed a world of meaning. She had not been sitting at his side in helpless pain, looking with fearful eyes into the dreary future when she should be alone and dependent with her child in a cold, selfish world. Forgetting her own heart-break, she had been untiring in her efforts to brighten his pathway down into the dark valley with the hope of heaven. God had blessed her angel work, for he seemed a Christian. I went away from that bedside more awed than if I had come from the presence of a king.

" Early one morning I was hastily summoned to the ward. It was crowded and confused. The last hours had now come. The artery had broken away beyond remedy, and from the ghastly wound the poor man's life-blood poured away in torrents, crimsoning the floor far and near. His face was pale and wild, for death had come at last in an awful form. In mistaken kindness they had kept his wife from him, fearing the effect of the scene upon her. Drawn by her frantic cries to the ward-master's room, I went and said to her — ' My poor friend, you can go to your husband, but for his sake you must be perfectly calm. We can do nothing for him if he is excited.' For his sake, ah! yes, for his sake she could do anything, even master the whirlwind of sorrow at her heart. In a moment she became as quiet and gentle as a lamb, and crept noiselessly to his side. The man rallied and lived a short time, and husband and wife were left alone. We may well draw the veil over that last solemn farewell.

"For a brief space the pair sat on the shores of time, the extreme cape and promontory of life. All around rolled the ocean of eternity. Then one went forward into the unknown, and the curtain between the two worlds fell. In wild agony she clasped his lifeless form. The ward-master sought tenderly to lift her and lead her away. For a moment the tempest in her soul found expression and she sprang upon him like a tigress. Then came again the strange, unnatural calm like that when the Master said, 'Peace, be still!' Quietly, thoughtfully she made all her arrangements and soon went northward to her dying mother, taking the precious dust of him she had loved with her, and we saw her no more. But her sad, pale, patient face will haunt me through life.

"If all the bits of romance in these hospitals were gathered up they would make volumes. I will instance only two cases.

"It is somewhat common to get shot now, and yet for all that it is none the less rather a painful and tragical experience. Well, two of our soldiers were shot; one had his arm taken off, and the other lost an arm and a leg also. They both wrote to their respective fair ones, expressing the fear that they would no longer wish to unite themselves with such mutilated specimens of humanity, and if such were their feelings they were free. The female engaged to the man who had lost an arm availed herself of his release. She could not think of marrying him under such circumstances. The blow was fatal to the poor fellow. He became hopelessly deranged, and is now in the asylum in this city. Still, considering her character, perhaps he escaped a worse fate.

"The lady engaged to the soldier who had lost both his arm and leg replied that she honored him for his wounds; that she loved him all the more for his patriotism and the heroism which led him to incur them; and that if he would permit her she would come on, and take care of him. She did so, and married him."

One turns with a feeling of relief, after the harrowing details in the letters already given, to this account of the Christmas festivities at Hampton Hospital.

"We are told that 'the desert shall blossom as the rose.' We believe it, for even the hospital, — the house of disease and wounds, the spot ever shadowed by the wings of the dark angel, — even this place of sombre associations can wreathe itself in festive garlands and resound with songs. Doctor McClellan, surgeon in charge, has the enlightened opinion that pills and physics are not the only health-restoring influences that can be brought to bear upon his patients. All efforts to celebrate the holidays with spirit have received his hearty sympathy and coöperation. The joyous season, so full of happy memories, has not passed in dull monotony. Though winds blew high and cold, still, throughout Thursday, Friday, and Saturday, the axes rang merrily in the woods. Huge masses of holly, cedar, and pine might be seen moving towards the different wards, and approaching near you would find a nurse or convalescent staggering along beneath the green and fragrant burden. Under the magic of many skilful hands the pliant boughs are soon tied and twisted into a thousand devices. Men with only one hand worked with the rest. Men possessing but a single leg were busy as the others. Thump, thump, over the floor go the crutches, as old battered veterans hobbled about in all directions, to view in different lights the artistic and fantastic results of their labors. Even the dull face of chronic pain lights up and wanly smiles, while dim eyes, fast closing on earthly scenes, gaze wistfully on the fragrant evergreens and query to themselves if they are to be the symbols of their memories at distant homes.

"But though many wards blossomed out into holiday garlands, the crowning glories of the kind were to be found in Ward C. Quaint devices, hanging festoons, wreaths and shields and graceful arches, draped the place in varied beauties like the tapestry of old, which turned rough and gloomy apartments into warm and silken bowers. The feathery cedar, tasselled pine, and far-famed laurel formed the rich background for the bright berries of the Christmas holly which glistened like rubies set in emerald folds. Flags were looped across the stage, and the curtains in the rear also showed the stars and stripes. The hospital choir and glee-club had here prepared an entertainment most agreeable to the tastes of all. Their motto, a beautiful transparency, explains its character, ' We come with songs to greet you.' As darkness fell a throng surrounded every door. Up the high steps to the main entrance, an hour before the doors were opened, crowding, jostling hundreds gathered, seeming like a human wave lifted by some powerful impulse from the sea of heads below. Around the building in circling eddies, knots of men sauntered talking, wondering, and anticipating concerning the pleasures of the evening. Above the swaying masses numerous crutches might be seen. Thus raised aloft they seemed like standards, showing well the spirit of our soldiers. It is not in wounds to keep them at home. If they have the sad misfortune not to

6

have two legs beneath them, they are sure to go on one if anything unusual calls them out. Within, now, the lamps are lighted, down the long and echoing ward, and through the festoons and glistening arches, they wink and twinkle like fireflies in a cedar forest. The doors are opened and, under Doctor McClellan's wise and careful supervision, at least a thousand persons are soon admitted and seated. Those not so fortunate as to get seats fill every space of standing room. The hall is full, and those who cannot gain admittance crowd around outside the windows, where faces gleam in the fitful light, like framed and grotesque pictures.

"At a given signal the orchestra commenced, and the hum and buzz of many voices died away like a breeze in the forest. But it is useless to attempt to describe music — songs and anthems that seem like living spirits which by powerful spells may be called up to float and pass before you, and stir the soul with magic influences. It was no rude affair. Ears that have been educated at the Academy of Music would have tingled with novel and delightful sensations, could they have heard those deep, rich soldiers' voices accompanied by our lady nurses, and the lady teachers of the Tyler House, chanting our national anthems, or exciting irresistible mirth by their comic songs. Mr. Tilden's ripe, powerful, mellow voice moved every heart, and more than satisfied the nicest and most critical ear. Mr. George Terry, changeful as an April day, now convulsed the audience with laughter, and again, a moment afterwards, caused all eyes to overflow. Mrs. Meachann, Miss Eastman, Mr. Sears, and Mr. Allen sustained their parts with marked ability, and little Miss Mary White brought down the house by singing a ballad whose simple beauty was universally appreciated. But where all perfectly performed the parts assigned to them, it is almost invidious to make distinctions. Mr. Metcalf, the leader of the choir, must have been satisfied with the performances, as certainly all others were. 'Home, Sweet Home,' closed the entertainment, and carried us all back to that dear and never-to-be-forgotten place. Again in fancy we gathered around the familiar hearthstone, made warm and bright by blazing fire and sweet memories of other days. God grant that another Christmas day may find us all there.

"But in the hospital there were hundreds confined by sickness, wounds, and weakness to their beds. However good their will may have been they were physically unable to join with their more fortunate companions in outside enjoyments. They were not forgotten or neglected. On Sab-

bath afternoon the choir again assembled, and
commencing with Ward One, we passed through
fourteen wards, making the old walls ring again
with Christmas anthems. This, with wishing the
patients a merry Christmas, and that another return of the happy day might find them all safe at
home, and the reading, in Luke ii., of the angelic
announcement to the shepherds of the 'unspeakable gift' to us all, constituted the simple service.
On Monday there was much high feeding. Sleek
cattle and corpulent pigs were roasted whole, and
there was a powerful mortality in the hospital
poultry-yard. Men who could never carve their
fortunes showed wonderful ability in carving tur-
key. These substantial luxuries, seasoned by the
recent victories, made for us a royal feast, to which
the sovereigns in blue sat down with unmingled
satisfaction."

CHAPTER VI

THE HOSPITAL FARM AND CHAPEL

IN a letter to the Hon. William Cullen Bryant, then editor of the *Evening Post*, Edward gives an account of the establishment of his hospital farm, and tells of its benefit to the men under his care.

"HON. WILLIAM C. BRYANT — DEAR SIR: The meeting in behalf of 'New York's disabled soldiers' has deeply interested me and awakened many war memories. During the last two years of the Rebellion I had some experience, in a small way, which may suggest useful features in a Soldiers' Home. At that time I was one of the chaplains of the Fortress Monroe hospitals, and the campaigns in the vicinity of Petersburg and Richmond often filled our long barracks to repletion and also covered the adjacent acres with temporary tent wards. Lying around the hospital there was an abundance of idle and unfenced land. With the sanction of Doctor McClellan, the surgeon in charge, I had this enclosed and planted with such vegetables as were most useful and conducive to health, the odorous onion taking the lead. The tulip mania had its day, but the weakness of average humanity for this bulb is as old as history — see Numbers xi., 5 — and apparently it is only growing more prevalent with the ages. If this is evolution in the wrong direction Mr. Huxley should look after it.

"The labor of the hospital farm was performed by the patients themselves, and very many soon became deeply interested in their tasks. When a man became so far convalescent from illness or wounds as to be able to do a little work, he was detailed for the garden and employed in its lighter labors. As he grew stronger he was put at heavier work. Heroes who had lost arms and legs supplemented each other's deficiencies, the two maimed men contriving to do between them far more than many a stout fellow who now demands $1.50 a day. A man with one hand could sow seed and weed the growing vegetables, while his comrade hitched along on his crutch and vigorously hoed the ground between the rows. I sometimes had as many as a hundred men at work, and I ever found that such tasks benefited body and soul. It did one's heart good to see pallid faces grow brown and ruddy, and flabby muscles round and hard. It did one more good thus easily to banish home-sickness and the miserable incubus of *ennui* from which the sufferer is prone to seek relief in some form of vicious excitement. For the satisfaction of those who ask for more practical results I can state that we were able to send green vegetables to the hospital kitchens by the wagonload. As the record of the second year at the farm, made at the time, I find among other items the following: 700 bushels of snap beans in the pod, 120 do. lima beans, 130 do. carrots, 125 do. peas, 470 do. potatoes, 250 do. tomatoes, 1,500 bunches of green onions, 30,000 heads of cabbage, 26,900 ears of sweet corn, 2,500 muskmelons, etc. A large poultry yard, enclosing four acres, was also built, and many other improvements made, all being accomplished by the willing labor of the convalescents themselves, who more rapidly regained their strength while thus furnishing the means of health to those still confined within the walls.

" Recalling these facts I am greatly pleased to learn that the ' New York Home ' is to be located on a farm, for thus it may be made a *home* in reality. Providence put the first man into a garden, and few men have lived since who have not felt more at home when a garden lay about the door."

During the years that Edward was at Hampton Hospital, his friend Mr. Merwin was doing a noble work among the soldiers in the hospitals at the front, under the direction of the Christian Commission.   My brother at one time wished to be relieved of his duties as chaplain for several weeks, and Mr. Merwin kindly consented to take his place. He afterwards wrote of this time : —

" I found that Edward's presence among the sick and wounded was sadly missed, and that he had labored in many ways to contribute to their comfort and happiness.   He brought from the North an experienced farmer and supplied the hospital with an abundance of excellent vegetables. Subsequently a church was erected by his efforts for the growing needs of that post."

While absent at the North my brother raised most of the funds necessary to build this chapel at Hampton.   When he revisited the place years afterward, he found the chapel still in use.   He was gratified also to learn that the hospital library continued to be of service.   He says:

" Some of us rode out to the former site of the hospital.   Many pleasant changes have occurred. The acres of ground occupied by sick and wounded men are now covered with orchards and the homes of peaceful industry.   The hospital garden has in part become the grounds of a college for freedmen, and is in a high state of cultivation.   The college itself is a fine building, and under the able, energetic administration of General Armstrong, is full of promise for the race that we have so long kept in ignorance. He is teaching them many things of vital use, and among these one of the most important is a wise, economical culture of the ground. The chapel to which we have referred is inclosed within the cemetery grounds, and only needs a few repairs now and then, to preserve it a substantial church for many years to come. I was told that there had been religious services in it nearly every Sabbath since the war.

" The soldiers' monument, now seen for the first time, impressed me most favorably. In its severe simplicity it truthfully commemorates the lives and characters of those who sleep beneath. Over three hundred dollars was given to me by the soldiers in twenty-five and fifty cent stamps and one-dollar bills, and with some these gifts were almost like the widow's mite — all they had. It was most gratifying to see how nobly their wish and purpose had been carried out. That it has been so is due to that friend of the soldier and of all humanity, Miss D. L. Dix, who to the mites of the hospital patients added thousands of dollars collected elsewhere."

From another letter I take Edward's description of the chapel.

" The building is cruciform in its shape, and at the foot rises a light and graceful tower and spire, sixty feet high, surmounted by a cross showing

each way.   The style of architecture is Gothic.
The chapel-room is thirty feet by sixty, with a high,
arched ceiling.   It is beautifully and smoothly
plastered, and whitened with some kind of hard
finish.   Two aisles run down the room, thus making three tiers of seats.   These are somewhat
Gothic in their form, and are stained black-walnut,
surmounted by a white round moulding, which
makes a pleasing contrast.   In the place where
the head of the cross should have been, there is
merely a small projection from the main building,
forming in the large chapel-room an alcove or re-
cess.   A beautiful Gothic frame containing two
medium-sized and one large window of stained
glass forms the rear of this projection, and aids in
lighting the room.   All the windows in the chapel
part are of stained glass, and they render the light
very soft and pleasant.   I found them about as
cheap as curtains, and much more pretty and
durable.   The space in the alcove is occupied by
a slightly raised platform and a plain, simple pulpit,
still lacking a cushion.   It is a very easy room
to speak in, and in it music sounds remarkably
well.   The left arm of the cross, towards the hospital, constitutes the library, and is a large, airy
room, thirty feet by twenty-four, furnished with
tables, book-shelves, and reading-desks.   Our collection of books is said to be one of the finest in

the hospital service. Here also will be found the magazines, dailies, and weeklies, and prominent among our files will be *The Evangelist*. The right arm of the cross consists of four small but pleasant rooms, and will now be used as the chaplain's quarters, and at some future time as a parsonage.

" The building is of a dark color, with white doors and window-frames. Around the entire structure has been built a rustic Gothic fence, constructed of smooth pine poles, and forming a heart-shaped enclosure. Therefore we have the following device: the church in the centre of the heart."

Soon after Edward's return from the North to his work at the hospital there was a marked revival of religion among the sick and wounded men. He says: —

" I think the most marked feature of the revival is the reclamation of those who have gone astray — who have found the temptations of camp life too powerful to be resisted. Since I have been in the service I have met hundreds of soldiers who acknowledged that they had been professors of religion at home. They had entered the army with the best of intentions, but the lack of Sabbath privileges, of the sacred influences of the hearth, and all the numberless aids which bolster up a church member at the North, together with the strong and positive allurements to sin in the field, had discovered to them their weakness and they had fallen. But in most cases it would seem that the old vital spark still smouldered at the bottom of their hearts. According to their own confessions, they are restless and dissatisfied, and unable to attain to the stolid or reckless apathy of those who have never tasted of the heavenly manna. Put them under the influence of an earnest prayer-meeting or faithful sermon, and they are like old rheumatic flies in an April sun, or the apparently dead and leafless trees in the warm breath of spring, or the veteran soldier who hears the familiar call to arms after years of ignoble peace. It is very interesting to watch them in our meetings. The first evening they take seats far back, and look around with an uneasy air, as if almost ashamed to be seen. The next evening they sit near the leader. They soon venture to respond faintly to some of the more earnest prayers. At last, unable to restrain the rising tide of feeling, they rise up, and often with tears and penitence confess their backslidings, resolve to be faithful hereafter, and ask the prayers of all present that they may never be so weak as to wander again. They then take their places amongst those whom I call the fighting part of the congregation — those whose active aid I can rely upon.

"In one of the wards, where 'the straightforward Christian' (as I call him) is on duty, they are having a little revival by themselves. He gives its inmates no peace till they become Christians in self-defence. During the beautiful moonlight nights of last month, he organized a little prayer-meeting, which met on the banks of an arm of the bay that runs up into the mainland near the ward, and there claimed and verified the promise of 'Where two or three are gathered together in My name, there am I in the midst of them.'

"God does seem near the soldiers, and the soldiers as a general thing are ready to respond to His gracious invitations, not only here but elsewhere, and in fact in every place where Christians are willing to come down, or rather up to their level, and work among them with a genuine, heartfelt sympathy.

"In a recent letter from the front, my brother, Rev. Alfred C. Roe, Chaplain 104th N. Y. V., writes: 'We have weekly and almost daily conversions. Our prayer-meetings, though held in the trenches, and often in close proximity to the enemy, are largely attended, and unless prevented by important business the colonel is always present. The staff at headquarters is like a Christian family.'

"I have found by experience that the formal pres-

entation of Gospel truth once a week by an officer in chaplain's uniform, or in any other, does
not amount to much, unless faithfully followed up
by personal effort and the social prayer-meeting.
The religion of our Saviour, presented in the spirit
of our Saviour, rarely fails to move even the rough
soldier.   I have found a most efficient colaborer
in Chaplain Billingsly, also in Chaplain Raymond."

CHAPTER VII

PASTORATE AT HIGHLAND FALLS

SOON after the close of the war Edward accepted a call to the little church at Highland Falls, about a mile below West Point. This was his only charge, and here he spent nine happy, useful years. His first impressions of the church and congregation may be gathered from the following letter.

"I found myself in a true orthodox Presbyterian church, for although the thermometer stood far below zero and the roads were snowy and unbroken, still the number of ladies present far exceeded that of the gentlemen. I regarded this fact as a good omen, for if a pastor can depend upon a few strong-hearted women (not strong-minded in the cant sense of the phrase), he has only to go forward prudently to certain success. Summing up the entire congregation, small and great, it nearly made that number so well known, alas, in country churches, which is appropriately termed 'a handful.'

" These good people were thinly scattered over

a plain little audience room that would seat comfortably one hundred and twenty. The church was bitter cold, and the situation of the pulpit, between the two doors, seemed designed to chill anything like enthusiasm on the part of the speaker. The construction of the building bore evidence that some architect of the olden time determined to achieve celebrity, in that he placed its back toward the street, and faced it toward nothing in particular. This, with minor eccentricities, really entitled the edifice to the antiquarian's attention. But I intend not a disrespectful word against the little church, for precious souls have been gathered there and trained for heaven."

It was in February that Edward received a unanimous call to this church, and from that time he gave himself up to the work of collecting funds for the erection of a new building. The majority of the people were not wealthy and many of them were very poor, but they did all they possibly could, many giving at the cost of great personal sacrifice. The brunt of the enterprise, however, necessarily fell upon my brother. About this time he began giving lectures on his experiences in the Civil War, often travelling many miles to deliver them, going wherever there was a chance to make money and so help forward his cherished object. He also obtained large sums from wealthy city churches and from friends, through personal solicitation.

At the end of two years Edward and his co-workers felt justified in laying the corner-stone of the new church.   Here is his description of the ceremony.

" Patient effort seldom fails of its reward, and the day we had long toiled and prayed for, when we could lay the corner-stone of our new church, at length arrived.   The 16th of September dawned, cloudy and dubious, like the commencement of the enterprise.   The morning hours brought dis-appointment and heavy rain, as the two long years of work and waiting had brought many discour-agements.   Rev. Dr. William Adams of New York, who was to have made the address, was unavoid-ably detained; and the skies frowned so darkly it was thought best to defer the ceremony.   But before the hour appointed there was a general brightening up.   The clouds broke away and van-ished over Crow Nest and the adjoining mountains. The sun smiled out in irresistible invitation and the people gathered in such numbers that it was thought best to go forward with the ceremony. This we were most anxious to do, as the North River Presbytery had honored our church as the place of its Fall meeting, and most of its members could upon this day be present with us.

" As the shadows were lengthening eastward, we gathered among the evergreens that surround the solid foundation of the new edifice. It was just such a gathering as we love to see at a church — representatives from every age and class in the community. Little barefooted urchins climbed up into the cedars and looked on with wondering eyes. All right! the church is as truly for them as for the President, should he honor us with a visit. In a huge block of granite at the northeast corner of the building a receptacle had been cut. Around this we gathered. The Hon. John Bigelow, our former Minister to France, commenced the simple ceremony with a very happy address. In simple periods of classic beauty he spoke of church edifices as the highest and most disinterested expressions of the benevolence and culture of a community; and in words that were good omens of the future he dwelt upon the beneficent influences flowing therefrom. The Pastor next came forward, and stated that a copy of the Scriptures *only*, as published by the American Bible Society, would be deposited in the stone. In this solemn and emblematic act we wished to leave out everything that would take from the simplicity and force of the figure. God's Word alone in its purity should underlie the material structure, and so we hoped His Word alone, unmixed and undistorted by human opinions, would be the foundation of the spiritual church that should be built there in coming years. Therefore no papers, coins, or records of any kind, were placed in the sealed box with the Bible. If after the lapse of centuries this solid wall were taken down, this solitary Bible, unmarred by pen or pencil, will be a clearer record than long and formal documents, of a church that sought to honor God, and not man, and to keep His name before the people, and not that of some human instrument. With the usual words the massy block of granite was lowered to its place, and, humanly speaking, generations will pass away before these leaves again are turned.

"The Rev. Dr. Wheeler of Poughkeepsie, who kindly offered to act in Dr. Adams's place, spoke in a vein of strong original eloquence which chained the attention of all for a brief time. As an impromptu effort it was singularly appropriate and hope-inspiring. He closed with a prayer, in the fervor of which a lady said that she could almost see the walls and spire rising to beautiful and entire completion. Rev. Mr. Teal of Cornwall pronounced the benediction, and thus closed the ceremony.

"We are building of the blue granite found in abundance upon the ground. The walls rise from the rocky foundation in massive thickness of plain, hammer-dressed stone, and thus are in keeping with the rugged mountain scenery. Time will rather strengthen the work than weaken it. We build from the rock with the rock, and trust that the great Spiritual Rock will underlie it all.

"It will cost us twenty thousand dollars to complete the church, and of this sum we have on hand, or promised, nearly half. The building is under contract to be finished the first of June next, and whatever indebtedness there exists will be provided for by a mortgage. The ladies of the church and the Sabbath-school children have pledged themselves by fairs and concerts to provide for the interest of the debt until the principal is paid. The people are proving that they are in earnest by their deeds. By their hearty sympathy and coöperation, Mr. Cozzens, the proprietor of the hotel, and his lady have greatly contributed to our success.

"The guests of the house have been very liberal and attentive, and show an increasing interest in the enterprise. At a time of hesitancy and doubt a generous gift of five hundred dollars, from C. K. Garrison, Esq., of New York, soon after followed by five hundred dollars more from Richard Schell, Esq., enabled us to go forward with hope and confidence. Mr. Garrison is a native of our region, and happy would it be for the country if, following his example, those who have won wealth and distinction abroad would return and enrich their birthplace by such noble proofs of their benevolence. Monuments of this kind perpetuate one's name better than tombstones. Among the summer worshippers at our little church under the trees, we have been glad to recognize so long the ·kindly face of Rev. J. G. Craighead of *The Evangelist*, and long and gratefully will our people remember his words from the pulpit and in the social meeting. Rev. Dr. Robinson of Harrisburgh, Pa., has also been one of our summer residents, and one that we shall soon sadly miss."

Four years longer minister and people worked unceasingly in the interests of their new church, my brother continuing to give his lectures wherever opportunity offered. One delivered at Providence, Rhode Island, was quoted at some length in a daily paper of that city, and is here reprinted.

"The Rev. E. P. Roe, of West Point, lectured last night before a fair audience, at Harrington's Opera House, under the auspices of Prescott Post No. 1, G. A. R., on 'Secret Service at the Front; or Scouting and Guerrillas.' During the war, said the speaker, the northern people regarded guerrillas as irresponsible bands of outlaws, living by violence and plunder, and while leaning to and assisting the rebels, ready to murder and rob with-

out much regard for either side. The majority of
the guerrillas were, no doubt, as bad as generally
supposed, but there were among them trusty and
intelligent scouts, whose employment was to trace
out the position and movements of the Union army,
and who, no matter how much robbing and murdering they might do on their own account, never
lost sight of the main object of their service. The
acuteness of these scouts and the various disguises
which they assumed were more than surprising.
As a division of the Union army passed along, an
old citizen might have been seen building a rail
fence. Surely that ancient-looking farmer knows
nothing, the passing troops would readily think.
But under that old felt hat gleamed a watchful eye
and listened attentive ears, observing and hearing
everything worthy of remark. As soon as the
army passed, he throws down his rails and slips off
to the swamp, mounts a fleet horse, and soon the
numbers, destination and condition of the Union
division are reported at the nearest rebel headquarters. Sometimes the woods on both sides
of the marching column swarmed with prowling
guerrillas; sometimes an affable stranger in Union
colors would approach, enter into conversation
with the weary straggler, gain all the information
he could, and then shoot down his informant.
They were very bold in their operations. One day

an orderly was riding with important despatches far within the Union lines, when he was startled by a mounted rebel, who made his appearance from the woodside, and who, presenting a pistol at his breast, demanded his arms and despatches. After, as he imagined, cleaning out the orderly, the rebel invited him to come along and accept a little Southern hospitality. The scout rode a little forward, and as he did so, a quiet grin played stealthfully over his furious countenance; a little pistol was withdrawn from a side pocket, the cold muzzle applied to the rebel's ear, and in a very few moments the rebel was disarmed and on his way to a Northern prison. But the bold deeds of the rebels in scouting through the Union lines paled before the achievements of General Sharpe and his bureau of military information. The promotion of this bureau was recommended by General Butterfield to General Hooper, in 1863, for the purpose of ascertaining the numbers, positions, and intentions of the enemy. To this bureau was gathered all the information of the signal corps and of the hundreds of scouts and spies who traversed the rebel army and country. Trusty and intelligent men were picked from the rank and file of the army and placed under command of General Sharpe. The first piece of work undertaken by the general was to obtain a full roster of Lee's

army as it lay on the Rappahannock, the numbers
and titles of regiments and the names of the corps,
division, brigade, regimental and company commanders.   He picked out General Heath's brigade
of A. P. Hill's corps as the first one to operate on,
and by daringly scouting in person through the
lines of that brigade, conversing with its pickets,
and mingling with its men, he succeeded in obtaining not only a full list of its officers, and an accurate detail of its strength, but a correct description
of the personal appearance and habits of these
officers.   After mastering Heath's division he
picked out an intelligent soldier whom he crammed
with all he knew himself about the division, dressed
him up in a rebel uniform, and sent him into another
division of Hill's corps.   Of course the man was at
once apprehended and taken before a provost marshal, but made such a plain statement, giving the
names of the officers of the regiments in Heath's
division, to which he claimed to belong, and describ-
ing their personal appearance and habits with more
accuracy than reverence, that he was dismissed,
with a reprimand for his want of respect for his
superior officers, and ordered to report back at once
to his regiment.   After looking around him and ascertaining everything worth noting with regard to
the command, he returned to General Sharpe; and
thus the particulars, as ascertained by every new

scout, facilitated the means of getting more. At
length Sharpe had a roster of the whole of Lee's
army, and could tell its strength at any time within
a thousand or so, that thousand being the changing
mass of stragglers, furloughed, and sick, to whom
no special location could be assigned. He could
also tell the name of every officer in that army,
and rebel generals of divisions might have gone to
him for information concerning their own subordi-
nates. The great usefulness of thus possessing the
precise knowledge of the strength and formation
of the enemy's forces was particularly illustrated
at Gettysburg, where the anxious spirits of the
Union commanders were relieved by ascertaining
from General Sharpe that every brigade but one
of Lee's army had been engaged in the fight, and
that that general had no reserve with which to
follow success or break defeat. Not least among
the resources from which valuable information
was obtained were the contrabands, whose fidelity
and truthfulness were remarkable, considering
their want of education, and consequent lack of
intelligence.

" Amusing and interesting instances were given
by the speaker of the hairbreadth escapes and
reckless daring of General Sharpe's scouts, and he
concluded an entertaining discourse by paying a
hearty and well-deserved tribute to their patriotic

and fearless devotion, to which was greatly owing,
in his opinion, the winning of some of our greatest
victories, and the fortunate issue of the war itself."

In 1868 the church was completed, a building
"whose granite walls are so thick, and hard-wood
finish so substantial, that passing centuries should
add only the mellowness of age." Edward would
not allow his name deposited in the corner-stone,
as many wished, but since his death a bronze tablet, with the following inscription, has been placed
in the vestibule.

In Memoriam,
Rev. Edward Payson Roe,
Minister of the
First Presbyterian Ch. of the Highlands.
1866–1875.
Author, Pastor, Friend,
This Building Stands the Monument of
His Earnest Labors.
Erected :
1868.

After the completion of the church the old parsonage was enlarged and remodelled, and so during
his pastorate thirty thousand dollars were raised
and expended in permanent improvements.

While living at Highland Falls Edward continually met the officers and soldiers of West Point.
A soldier at one time was the leader of his choir,

in which was also a quartet from the military band. He writes as follows of a mountain camp at West Point which recalled some of his own army life : —

" About the middle of August the Cadet Corps left their airy tent villas on the plain at West Point, and took up their line of march for the mountains. The pioneers had preceded, and the road was practicable not only for infantry, but for carriages and stages laden with fair ladies from the hotels. The selected camping ground, though rough indeed compared with the velvet lawns of West Point, was admirably adapted for the purpose. It was a broken, uneven field, on the property of T. Cozzens, Esq. Here in the midst of the wildest mountain scenery the young soldiers experienced, to quite an extent, the realities of life at the front, minus the element of danger. But the mimicry was almost perfect, and so suggestive of bygone days to an old campaigner, that I cannot refrain from indulging in a brief description.

" A wild, romantic drive of three or four miles through winding valleys, jagged boulders and ledges, and overshadowing trees, brought us to the edge of the camp-ground. Along the road ran the familiar military telegraph, the wire now looped up to a convenient tree, now sustained by the slender portable pole that bends but never breaks beneath the seemingly gossamer strand.

Just before reaching the place we struck off upon one of those temporary roads that we were ever extemporizing in Virginia.   First we saw the white tents through the foliage, then the gleaming of a sentry's musket, the cover of an ambulance, and in a moment more we were in the midst of the encampment, and the spell was complete.   Through the strong laws of association the old life rushed back again, and what often seems a far-away dream was as present and real as six years ago.   But apart from all its suggestiveness to those who dwelt in canvas cities and engaged in war's realities, the scene was novel, beautiful, and deeply interesting. Here in the midst of the wooded highlands was a fac-simile, reproduced in miniature, of thousands of encampments, created by the Rebellion, in the equally wild regions of the Southern States.   Here were our future generals learning to apply practically to the roughness of nature the principles and tactics that might seem comparatively easy on paper or grassy plain.   Sloping down to the right, the encampment bordered on Round Pond, a beautiful, transparent little lake, fringed with water-lilies, and mirroring back the rocks and foliage of its rugged banks.   Through the courtesy of Mr. Cozzens we and others were soon skimming its surface in an airy little pleasure boat.   A quarter of a mile to the left, in full view, with a descent of a hundred

feet, Long Pond glistened in the bright August
sun. All around rose the green billowy hills as
far as the eye could reach. We had hardly noted
this beautiful commingling of wood and water
before the stirring notes of the drum announced
skirmish drill. On each side of the camp a squad
marched briskly out, and was soon lost in the forest. Soon from its unseen depths there came a
shot, then another, then several, ending in a rapid,
scattering fire, and I was back again on the skirmish line in Virginia. By this time the other detachment had reached position, and were 'popping'
away in the old familiar style. The hills caught up
the reports and echoed them down again multiplied
a hundredfold.

> " Rock, glen, and cavern paid them back ;
>   To many mingled sounds at once,
>   The awakened mountain gave response ; "

and these regions of silvan peace and solitude were
disturbed as they never had been since the days
when Washington made West Point his military
base, and Fort Putnam was the chief Highland
stronghold.

"On a high eminence to the right fluttered a
signal flag. I shall never forget the last time that
my special attention was called to that very significant object. It was on a bold ledge of the Blue

Ridge west of Culpepper, Va. We were out on picket, lounging away a long bright October afternoon, when in the far distance a white flutter like that of a lady's handkerchief caught the wary eye of the colonel. Listlessness vanished. All glasses were out, but practised eyes discovered, not a token of ladies' favor, but a signal of stern war. Lee was turning our right flank, and then followed the famous race for Centreville heights.

"But the sun had sunk behind a blue Highland, and the tap of the drum announcing parade recalled from reminiscences of the past. Creaking, groaning, crunching up the rough road came stages, carriages, and wagons of all descriptions laden with fair ladies, who in bright summer costumes seemed airy indeed, but from the looks of the jaded horses, were anything but thistle-downs. The wild mountain camp was soon brilliant with Fifth Avenue toilets. There was a general 'presenting of arms,' though not with belligerent aspect, and it required no astrologer to predict a conjunction of Mars and Venus. Old fogy that I was, recalling the days of our humdrum soldiering long and well gone by, here I was in the midst of a brilliant active campaign, where wounds were given and received, human hearts pierced to the very circumference — perhaps deeper sometimes. Yon tall, soldierly figure of the commandant is a sec-

ondary one here. Cupid is the field marshal of
the day. With the near approach of night there
was a suspension of hostilities. The fair invaders
gradually drew off their attacking forces, and soon
were lost in the deeper shadows that lay at the
mountain base. The next morning at 8 A. M.,
the Cadet Corps returned to their encampment on
the plain at West Point."

My brother's attitude toward West Point is
clearly shown in the following vigorous defence
of the National Academy which was published in
The Evangelist.

"The Military Academy here has lately had an
unenviable degree of notoriety and of severe criticism. Some go so far as to advise the breaking
up of the entire institution. No one so thought
when the gallant Reynolds at the cost of his life
made such vigorous battle at Gettysburg as to
check Lee, and secure to us a favourable position
for fighting out the decisive conflict of the war.
No one so advised when a graduate of West Point
announced the surrender of Vicksburg; when another marched from Atlanta to the sea; and another swept down the Shenandoah Valley like a
whirlwind. During our national struggle for life,
trained soldiers did for us what educated lawyers,
physicians, clergymen, and statesmen do for a community at all times. Next to the courage and pa-

triotism of the people, we have to thank the skill of West Point, that we are One Nation to-day.

There are those who advocate State military schools, in other words that we have an army officered by men of local interests and feelings. We shall then have generals to whom a single State is more than the whole Union. We shall have patriots educated by the New York ring, and the champions of Tammany Hall. No, the soldiers and sailors of the United States — as they are in the service of the whole country — should be educated by the whole country, and upon their maps State boundaries should be blotted out.

"Others advise, instead of this National Academy, that a course of military instruction be added to our colleges. But in this way students would only pick up a smattering of military science, in connection with a dozen other sciences, that would be quite useless in time of war. If we are to be fully armed against attack, we need men thoroughly educated in military science by the Nation, and therefore bound by every instinct of honor, gratitude, and association to defend her in her hour of peril.

"Does West Point now furnish such an education and such men? Yes, as truly as it ever has done; and I think it could be shown that it was never in better condition than it is this day. But

what does the recent ' outrage ' indicate, and what
the ' persecution of Cadet Smith ? ' Living near
the institution, and yet having no connection with
it — nothing to gain or lose — I can form as correct and unprejudiced an opinion as those who
base theirs upon partial, imperfect reports of isolated incidents.   One needs but to visit the Point
daily, or nightly, in order to see that perfect discipline is maintained.   The ' outrage ' referred to
was the expelling of three students by the first
class.   This action no one defends.   From no
source have I heard it so severely condemned as
by the officers themselves.   If it could have been
foreseen it would have been prevented.   In the
most quiet communities there are sudden out-
breaks of passion and violence.   Is the community
where such an event occurs, and which goes on its
orderly way the remaining three hundred and
sixty-four days of the year, to be called ' lawless ? '   Is the hasty, passionate act of a few,
wrong as it may be, to give character to all?
Moreover, in judging acts we should consider
the motives.   In this case they throw much light on
the action.   The sentiment of the corps is one of
intense disgust at the vice of lying.   A cadet cannot commit a more serious offence against the received code of honor.   The parties expelled were
believed to have been guilty of this offence, and

8

their dismissal was a sudden and lawless expression of the general anger and disgust. The action was contrary to the character of a soldier — the man of discipline and iron rules. But was it contrary to the character of frank, impulsive youth? Are those who have scarcely reached their majority to be judged in the same light as cool, grey-bearded veterans? I do not see how the officers are to blame because they could not foresee the trouble. Is a careful housekeeper 'reckless' because a kerosene lamp explodes? Do you say she ought to use non-explosive material? Then you must send sexagenarians to West Point instead of boys.

"The same principle applies to the 'persecution.' Critical editors, and advanced politicians like Ben. Butler, require of a class of young men gathered from every part of the land what they could scarcely obtain from the reformers of New England as a body. There is no use in ignoring the general and widespread prejudice of race. Many who grieve most at the wrongs of the colored people still feel that instinctive drawing back from social contact. Do those that condemn the young men most severely introduce the colored element largely into their own social circles? If not, then they should not be so ready to throw stones. Colored cadets sent to West Point must be treated in precisely the same way as the others. The law forms them all into a social community with equal rights. Is it to be expected that the utmost cordiality should be shown by hot-blooded, unformed, and often unwise youth, having in somewhat intenser form the same prejudices with those who condemn them? They have probably acted in the matter very much as the sons of the editors and ministers and reformers, who have been so severe upon them, would have acted in like circumstances. That happy day when the brotherhood of the race shall be honestly and lovingly acknowledged I fear is yet far distant, nor is it to be hastened by attempting to force a social intercourse against which there may be a natural aversion. As far as the officers are concerned, I believe that they have tried to treat young Smith with strict impartiality, and to give him every opportunity. The affairs of the Academy seem to go forward like clock-work. Considering the sore and excited state of mind among the cadets, their order and subordination have been remarkable. Of course two hundred and fifty young men of the widest difference of chararacter, brought together from every diversity of life, could not be expected to act like nicely adjusted machines; but with the exception of those two affairs, what has there been to justify the charges of 'lawlessness' or 'looseness of discipline?'

"In view of its services, it is strange that any-one should speak seriously of breaking up West Point. It has paid back to the nation all that has been spent upon it a hundredfold.

"P. S.— May I add a word in regard to the commandant of this post, who is the officer who has special care of the students in the Academy. Political attacks do not spare anybody, and during the recent troubles slurs have been thrown out even against General Upton. It has been in-timated that fear of the authorities at Washington has made him over-lenient and slack in his dis-cipline toward the first class, as President Grant and others high in power have sons in this class.

"These disparaging remarks are made either by those who know nothing of General Upton's char-acter and antecedents, or else they are the gross-est slanders. Search the army through and it would be impossible to find a man more utterly devoid of the spirit that truckles to power. Nature never put into his composition the least spice of obsequiousness, and one has only to look into the man's face and hear him speak five words in order to know it. He belongs to that class of men who pay more attention to the poor and humble than to the high and haughty.

"I think my testimony in this matter is worth something. During nearly four years of life in the army, and five years' residence within one mile of the West Point Academy, I have met with a great many officers of the volunteer and regular service, and never has a man more thoroughly impressed me with the fact that he was a gentleman, and conscientious in duty even to the slightest particular, than General Upton. Moreover, he is an enthusiast in his profession, and therefore successful. He is the author of the Infantry Tactics now in use in our army, and said to be the finest in the world. From frequent intercourse with the Point, I know that he maintains a daily discipline among the cadets as nearly perfect as anything of the kind can be. It is my belief that investigation of the recent troubles will show that the institution was never better officered than at present.

"Moreover, General Upton is a sincere Christian — one that lives up to his profession. His influence in this respect is most marked and happy upon the corps. We cannot overestimate the importance of the fact that the officer directly in charge of the young men at the Point is guided in all respects, not only by strict military honor and duty, but by the highest Christian principle."

CHAPTER VIII

RESIGNATION FROM THE MINISTRY

WHILE at Highland Falls Edward wrote his first novel, "Barriers Burned Away." He had told of his plan for a story to be based upon the scenes he had witnessed among the ruins of the great Chicago fire, and when I received a letter from him the following winter asking me to make him a visit as soon as possible, I suspected that he wanted my opinion of what he had written. And I was not disappointed, for on the evening after my arrival he read to me a number of chapters, and we talked over his plan for the story until after midnight, he going over the outlines that he then had in mind, though he afterward made some changes. The next day he called upon Dr. Field, editor of *The Evangelist*, and owing to his kind encouragement the visit was repeated, the result being that the story was finally accepted for serial publication in that paper.

From that time on, my brother read to me every one of his stories in manuscript, and I enjoyed them the more from the fact that in every case I recognized the originals from which he had drawn his scenes and characters, idealized as they were.

In 1874 his health had become so much impaired by overwork that his physician strongly urged him to give up either writing or preaching. After giving the matter serious consideration and consulting with friends whose advice he valued, my brother reluctantly decided to retire from the ministry. How his people parted with him is told in a letter to *The Evangelist*, whose readers had followed with so much interest and substantial aid my brother's efforts to build a new church.

" I have been very much surprised. Last Sabbath, the 7th of March, was my birthday. On the 6th I sat quietly in my study until the sun was behind the mountains, and then was sent out of the house on false pretences. The young people of the church were getting up an entertainment, and suddenly took it into their heads that they needed my assistance. There seemed many delays, but we at last got through. Then I received a startling message that a neighbor wished to see me immediately. Surmising sudden illness or trouble, I did not go home, but started off in great haste. I found not sickness, but mystery, at this neighbor's, which I could not fathom. My friend and his wife were unusually entertaining and I could not get away, though I knew I was keeping tea waiting at home. Finally there came another mysterious message — 'Two gentlemen and two ladies wished to see me at the parsonage.' 'O, I understand now,' I thought. 'It is a wedding; but they are managing it rather oddly.'

"But imagine my surprise when I opened the door, and found about one hundred and fifty people present. Well, to be brief, they just overwhelmed us with kindness. They gave us fine music, and provided a supper for five hundred instead of one hundred and fifty.

"Mrs. Roe thought that she was in the secret; but they surprised her also by presenting, with cordial words, a handsome sum of money at the close of the evening.

"My resignation has not yet been accepted, but we expect that the pastoral relation will be dissolved at the next meeting of Presbytery. As soon as spring comes in reality, and the embargo of ice and snow is over, we must be upon the wing; and this spontaneous and hearty proof of the friendliness of my people was very grateful to me. During the nine years of my pastorate they have been called to pass through many trying and difficult times. They have often been asked to give beyond their means, and have often done so. With the very limited amount of wealth in the congregation, even the generous aid received from abroad and from visitors could not prevent the effort to erect a new church and parsonage from being an exceedingly heavy burden, involving perplexing and vexatious questions. When I remember how patiently they have borne these burdens, how hard many have worked, and how many instances of genuine self-denial there have been, I feel that too much cannot be said in their praise. It is my hope and my belief that they will deal as kindly with my successor as they have with me."

Dr. Edgar A. Mearns of the United States army was one of my brother's devoted friends who knew him intimately during the years of his ministry. In 1888, from Fort Snelling, Minn., he writes as follows: —

" The sad news of the death of Rev. E. P. Roe, at Cornwall-on-Hudson, reached me to-day, and filled my heart with sadness. During the long years of my sojourn upon the western frontier, I have looked forward with unspeakable pleasure to the time when I could grasp the hand of this true friend, and walk and talk with him, and enjoy once more the society of his dear family. I had planned a leave of absence from my station in the desert-wilderness of Arizona for last spring, in response to his urgent invitations; but other duties awaited me, and I was not permitted to realize the fulfilment of this ardent desire. We were to walk through the woodlands, drive over the mountains, and sail on our native Hudson. I saw in mental vision the very rock under which we used to poke at the woodchucks with a stick, and on which we gathered the walking fern, and seemed once more to hear him discoursing of small fruits in his delightful garden, or reading to the family circle from his latest manuscripts. In the West many hearts have been pierced by this sorrow, for he made friends wherever he went.

" To write a word of the lost friend, who has been a very pillar of support in times of struggle or affliction, will perhaps relieve a pain at the heart which is hard to bear. It is not as an author, justly celebrated, that I must speak of him, but of the private life of one who combined every attribute of mind and heart to endear him to his friends. I have known him as a pastor, laboring assiduously among the members of his flock, dispensing liberal charity among the poor, and lightening everybody's burden. He was a rock to lay hold of when other friendships were borne away by the cruel winds of adversity. Then it was that the genial warmth of his smile, the kindly hand-pressure, and the cheerful encouragement of his voice fettered sore hearts to his.

"I have seen him as a hero, struggling in the water and broken ice, bearing in his arms the bodies of children for whom he risked his life. He had heard a cry for help, and that alone was enough to enlist the sympathy and secure the highest sacrifice of which our nature is capable. Then, paying no heed to personal sickness and injury, he strove to comfort the bereaved hearts of mothers, whose boys were drowned, perhaps by exposure laying the seeds of the disease which recently caused his death.

"His zealous devotion to his calling, together with exposure to various hardships encountered on frequent lecturing tours made for the purpose of obtaining funds for the erection of a suitable church for his congregation, made such inroads into his naturally vigorous constitution that, having accomplished his task, he was compelled to resign his charge as pastor, after about nine years of faithful service. The beautiful stone Presbyterian church at Highland Falls is a monument to his untiring efforts."

CHAPTER IX

FRUIT CULTURE AND LITERARY WORK

AFTER my brother's resignation from the ministry, he bought a plain, old-fashioned house with considerable ground about it, at Cornwall-on-the-Hudson, two miles distant from his childhood home, and went there to live.

It soon became evident, however, that Edward could not depend upon his literary work alone for the support of his growing family. He had for some years taken much interest in the cultivation of small fruits, and after the removal to Cornwall he carried on this work upon a larger scale, finding it profitable as well as interesting.

I remember the piles of letters that came to him each day for several years containing orders for plants. Although in general not a methodical man, yet the painstaking care which he was known to exercise in keeping the many varieties distinct enabled his customers to rely implicitly upon his statements as to the kind and value of the plants ordered. He often employed many men and boys on his place, but always engaged them with the understanding that if through carelessness the varieties of plants became mixed the offender was to be dismissed at once, and a few examples soon taught his assistants that he meant what he said. But when they were faithful to their duty, they invariably found him considerate and kind.

The strawberry was Edward's favorite among the small fruits, and he made many experiments with new varieties. When the vines were bearing, sometimes as many as forty bushels of berries were picked in a single day. Some of them were of mammoth size. I remember on one occasion we took from a basket four berries which filled to the brim a large coffee-cup, and notwithstanding their enormous size they were solid and sweet. During this period he wrote the articles on " Success with Small Fruits," published in *Scribner's Magazine*.

Currants came next in his favor. Writing of them he says: " Let me recommend the currant cure. If any one is languid, depressed in spirits, inclined to headaches, and generally ' out of sorts,' let him finish his breakfast daily for a month with a dish of freshly picked currants. He will soon doubt his own identity, and may even think that he is becoming a good man. In brief, the truth of the ancient pun will be verified, ' That the power to live a good life depends largely upon the *liver.*' Let it be taught at the theological seminaries that the currant is a means of grace. It is a corrective, and that is what average humanity most needs."

Mr. Charles Downing of Newburgh, a noted horticulturist, was Edward's valued friend. He was especially successful in fruit culture, and it was his custom to forward to my brother for trial novelties sent to him from every part of the country. Then on pleasant summer afternoons the old gentleman would visit my brother, and, side by side, they would compare the much-heralded strangers with the standard varieties. Often forty or fifty kinds were bearing under precisely the same conditions. The two lovers of Nature thus gained knowledge of many of her secrets.

Edward's coming to live in Cornwall was a source of great pleasure to our father, who, although then past eighty years of age, was still vigorous, and as full of enthusiasm for his garden as when he first moved to the country. Often on summer mornings, before the sun was fairly above the eastern mountains, father would drive over to my brother's, taking in his phaeton a basket of fruit or vegetables that he believed were earlier than any in my brother's garden. These he would leave at the front door for Edward to discover when he came downstairs, and return in time for our breakfast. He would laugh with the keenest enjoyment if he found that his beans or sweet corn had ripened first. Frequently he would remain at his son's house for breakfast, and afterwards the two would wander together over the grounds while the dew was still fresh upon the fruit and flowers. Many of the rosebushes and shrubs had been transplanted from the old garden, and it delighted my father and brother to see that they were flourishing and blooming in their new environment.

When Edward first moved to Cornwall several newspapers severely criticised him for giving up the ministry to write novels. I was sitting with him alone in his library one day when such a criticism came to him through the mail. After reading it he handed it quietly to me, went to his desk and took down a bundle of letters, saying: " These are mostly from young men, not one of whom I know, who have written to me of the benefit received from my books." He then read to me some of those touching letters of confession and thanks for his inspiring help to a better life.

When he finished reading the letters he said: " I know my books are read by thousands; my voice reached at most but a few hundred. I believe many who would never think of writing to me such letters as these are also helped. Do you think I have made a mistake? My object in writing, as in preaching, is to do good, and the question is, Which can I do best? I think with the pen, and I shall go on writing, no matter what the critics say."

Still his name was retained on the rolls of the North River Presbytery, and he was always ready to preach when needed, especially in neglected districts. For a long time after father's death he kept up the little Sunday-school that had been father's special care.

His home commanded a fine view of the river and mountains, and he would watch with great delight the grand thunder-storms that so often sweep over the Highlands. I take this description of a storm from one of his letters: —

"This moist summer has given a rich, dark luxuriance to the foliage, that contrasts favorably to the parched, withered aspect of everything last year. The oldest inhabitants (that class so sorely perplexed in this age of innovations) were astonished to learn that a sharp frost occurred in the mountains back of us, just before the Fourth. Even the seasons have caught the infection of the times, and no longer continue their usual jog-trot through the year, but indulge in the strangest extremes and freaks.

"A person living in the city can have little idea of thunder-storms as they occur in this mountain region. The hills about us, while they attract the electrified clouds, are also our protection, for,

VIEW FROM THE PIAZZA AT " ROELANDS."

abounding in iron ore, they become huge lightning-rods above the houses and hamlets at their bases. But little recks old Bear Mountain, or Cro' Nest, Jove's most fiery bolts. The rocky splinters fly for a moment; some oak or chestnut comes quivering down; but soon the mosses, like kindly charity, have covered up the wounded rock, and three or four saplings have grown from the roots of the blighted tree.

" But the storm we witness from our safe and sheltered homes is often grand beyond description. At first, in the distant west, a cloud rises so dark that you can scarcely distinguish it from a blue highland. But a low muttering of thunder vibrates through the sultry air, and we know what is coming. Soon the afternoon sun is shaded, and a deep, unnatural twilight settles upon the landscape like the shadow of a great sorrow on a face that was smiling a moment before. The thunder grows heavier, like the rumble and roar of an approaching battle. The western arch of the sky is black as night. The eastern arch is bright and sunny, and as you glance from side to side, you cannot but think of those who, comparatively innocent and happy at first, cloud their lives in maturer years with evil and crime, and darken the future with the wrath of heaven. At last the vanguard of black flying clouds, disjointed, jagged, the rough

9

skirmish line of the advancing storm, is over our heads. Back of these, in one dark, solid mass, comes the tempest. For a moment there is a sort of hush of expectation, like the lull before a battle. The trees on the distant brow of a mountain are seen to toss and writhe, but as yet no sound is heard. Soon there is a faint, far-away rushing noise, the low, deep prelude of nature's grand musical discord that is to follow. There is a vivid flash, and a startling peal of thunder breaks forth overhead, and rolls away with countless reverberations among the hills. In the meantime the distant rushing sound has developed into an increasing roar. Half-way down the mountain-side the trees are swaying wildly. At the base stands a grove, motionless, expectant, like a square of infantry awaiting an impetuous cavalry charge. In a moment it comes. At first the shock seems terrible. Every branch bends low. Dead limbs rattle down like hail. Leaves, torn away, fly wildly through the air. But the sturdy trunks stand their ground, and the baffled tempest passes on. Mingling with the rush of the wind and reverberations of thunder, a new sound, a new part now enters into the grand harmony. At first it is a low, continuous roar, caused by the falling rain upon the leaves. It grows louder fast, like the pattering feet of a coming multitude. Then the great drops fall around, yards apart, like scattering shots. They grow closer, and soon a streaming torrent drives you to shelter. The next heavy peal is to the eastward, showing that the bulk of the shower is past. The roar of the thunder just dies away down the river. The thickly falling rain contracts your vision to a narrow circle, out of which Cozzens's great hotel and Bear Mountain loom vaguely. The flowers and shrubbery bend to the moisture with the air of one who stands and takes it. The steady, continuous plash upon the roof slackens into a quiet pattering of raindrops. The west is lightening up; by and by a long line of blue is seen above Cro' Nest. The setting sun shines out upon a purified and more beautiful landscape. Every leaf, every spear of grass is brilliant with gems of moisture. The cloud scenery has all changed. The sun is setting in unclouded splendor. Not the west but the east is now black with storm; but the rainbow, emblem of hope and God's mercy, spans its blackness, and in the skies we again have suggested to us a life, once clouded and darkly threatened by evil, but now, through penitence and reform, ending in peace and beauty, God spanning the wrong of the past with His rich and varied promises of forgiveness. At last the skies are clear again. Along the eastern horizon the retreating storm sends up occasional flashes, that seem like regretful thoughts of the past. Then night comes on, cool, moonlit, breathless. Not a leaf stirs where an hour before the sturdiest limbs bent to the earth. This must be nature's commentary on the 'peace that passeth all understanding.'"

At this period Dr. Lyman Abbott made his permanent home in Cornwall, going almost daily to the city to attend to his duties as editor of the *Christian Union.*

In a short article written for that paper my brother describes a drive taken over the mountains when Dr. Abbott was entertaining the Brooklyn Association of Congregational Ministers.

" Pleasures long planned and anticipated often prove 'flat, stale, and unprofitable' when at last they disappoint us in their sorry contrast with our hopes, while on the other hand good times that come unexpectedly are enjoyed all the more keenly because such agreeable surprises. The other morning the editor of the *Christian Union*, Dr. Lyman Abbott, who is a near neighbor and a nearer friend, appeared at my door with the announcement that he was to meet on the morrow at the West Point landing the New York and Brooklyn Association of Congregational Ministers, at the same time giving me an invitation to accompany him, which I accepted on the spot. The morning of the 27th found us leading an array of carriages

up the Cornwall slope of the mountain, for it had
been arranged that the gentlemen whom Mr. and
Mrs. Abbott were to entertain for the day should
land at West Point and enjoy one of the finest
drives in America across the Highlands, instead of
a prosaic ride down from Newburgh through the
brickyards.   The Albany day boat was on time,
and so were we, and there stepped on shore a venerable body of divinity, or rather several bodies,
led by Rev. Henry Ward Beecher and his brother,
Dr. Edward Beecher.   A shower the previous
evening had left less dust than could be found in
the immaculate parlor of a spinster, and the heated
air had been cooled to such a nicety of adjustment
that we grew warm in the praise of its balminess.
With much good-natured badinage and repartee
we climbed the West Point hill and took the outer
avenue that skirts the river edge of the plain and
campus.   ' The brethren ' gazed with mild curiosity at ' Flirtation Walk ' where it led demurely
and openly from the main road, but soon lost itself in winding intricacies, mysterious copsewood,
and the still deeper mysteries suggested by the
imagination.   Let no grave reader lift a disdainful
nose.   Perhaps this same secluded path of frivo-
lous name has had a greater influence on human
destiny than himself.

" The trim plain and trimmer cadets were soon

left far behind, and nature began to wear the aspect it had shown to our great grandfathers when children. Through the skilful engineering of Mr. Charles Caldwell, a most excellent road of easy grades winds across Cro' Nest and Butter Hill (the latter was rechristened 'Storm King' some years since by the poet, N. P. Willis). As our path zigzagged up the shaggy sides of Cro' Nest, wider and superber views opened out before us, until at last West Point with its gleaming tents, the winding river with its silver sheen, and the village of Cold Spring lay at our feet, while to the southwest a multitude of green highlands lifted their crests like a confusion of emerald waves. A few moments more brought us to the summit, and although we were but a thousand feet nearer heaven than when we started, the air was so pure and sweet and the sky so blue that it might well seem to those who had so recently left the stifling city that they had climbed half-way thither. A half an hour's ride brought us to the northern slope of the mountains. Here we made a halt at Mr. Cobb's 'School on the Heights,' and were entertained with unlimited cherries, which by some strange providence had escaped the boys, and also by some exceedingly interesting gymnastic exercises that were performed to the rhythm of gay music. There are probaby few finer views on the river than that from Mr. Cobb's piazza and grounds, and thus his pupils are under the best of influences out of doors as well as within. As Mr. Abbott's guests looked down upon the broad expanse of Newburgh Bay, the city itself, the picturesque village of Cornwall, and the great swale of rich diversified country that lay between our lofty eyrie and the dim and distant Shawangunk Mountains that blended with the clouds, they must have felt indebted to their host for one of the richest pleasures of their lives.

"At last Mr. Beecher said that he carried an internal clock which plainly intimated that it was time for dinner. The *descensus* was easy, but Mrs. Abbott's warm welcome and hot dinner suggested an *avernus* only by blissful contrast. The fun, wit, and jollity of the remainder of the evening can no more be reproduced than the sparkle of yesterday's dew or the ripple of yesterday's waves. It was a pleasant thing to see those gray-haired men, many of whom had been burdened with care more than half a century, becoming boy-like again in feeling and mirthfulness."

During Edward's residence in Cornwall, each year about the middle of June, when the roses and strawberries were in their prime, it was his custom to send an annual invitation to the Philolethean Club of clergymen in New York City to visit him for a day at his home. Dr. Howard Crosby, Dr. Lyman Abbott, Dr. Schaeffer, and many other well-known clergymen were members of this club. At these meetings the learned and dignified clergymen threw aside all formality and were like a company of college boys off for a frolic. Their keen wit, quick repartee, and droll stories at these times will never be forgotten by those privileged to listen.

In 1882 heavy financial loss came upon us as a family owing to the failure of an elder brother. Edward, in his efforts to help him, became deeply involved, and to satisfy his creditors was obliged to sell the copyrights of several of his earlier books. These were bought by a friend without his knowledge at the time. After several years of incessant labor he worked his way out of these difficulties, and, owing to the immense sale of his books, was able to redeem his copyrights. He then felt free to take rest and change of scene in a trip to Southern California.

CHAPTER X

HOME LIFE

AS a matter of course, my brother had frequent calls from newspaper correspondents and others who were interested in, and curious about, the private life of a successful author. The first of the articles here quoted was entitled " A Talk with E. P. Roe," and was printed in a Brooklyn newspaper in 1886; the second appeared in a Detroit journal.

" The works of few novelists of the present day have had such remarkable sales as those of Mr. E. P. Roe, and this will be the more readily granted when it is known that one million copies of his novels have been sold in America alone, to which nearly one-half of that number may be added as representing their sale in England, Canada, Australia, and the different languages into which they have been translated.

" In appearance the novelist is a man of a trifle over the medium size, with a pleasant, intellectual face, which is almost covered with a rich and handsome coal-black beard and mustache. Mr.

Roe is in the prime of manhood, being about forty-five years of age, and his manners and conversation are the most kindly and engaging. He is of a generous disposition, hospitable, a kind friend, and never happier than when in the bosom of his family, to which he is devotedly attached.

"It was the pleasure of the writer a few evenings ago to meet the novelist and engage him in conversation regarding himself and his works.

"'I have just returned from an afternoon stroll,' remarked the novelist. 'This is my invariable custom after my day's work. When do I work? Well, I generally sit down immediately after breakfast, which I have about eight o'clock, and with the exception of an hour for lunch, I write continuously from that time until three or four in the afternoon. Then I go out for my walk.'

"'You never work at night, then?' was asked.

"'No; it is a bad practice, and one that I rarely indulge in. There was a time when I did so, but my work always showed it. A writer's work at night is almost always morbid. There is no better time to work than during the morning.'

"'How much work constitutes a day's labor with you?'

"'That varies a great deal. Sometimes I write four or five pages of foolscap, and other days I will write as much as fifteen. I have no average, but do as much as I feel like doing, or have time to do, and then I stop.'

"'Do you derive genuine pleasure from your work?'

"'Always, for I am absorbed in whatever I am writing. I presume I derived the most pleasure from my "Nature's Serial Story," for it was an out-of-door study, and anything about nature always finds a responsive chord in me. Then, two of the characters of that work portray my father and my mother, and their memory is blessed and sacred to me. All the other characters are imaginary.'

"'Are your stories and novels based on facts and real happenings, as a rule?'

"'In every case,' replied Mr. Roe. 'I never manufacture a story; I could n't do it. Of course, I elaborate and idealize, but the actual facts are always drawn from real life. I am always on the alert for these incidents, and when I see one that I think is adapted for a story I make a note of it.'

"'Speaking of your correspondence, like that of most authors, I presume it is of a various nature?'

"'Yes, indeed,' laughingly replied the novelist. 'It is surprising what letters I sometimes receive, and how difficult it is for some persons to realize that an author's time is valuable. Of course, I am not a stranger to the autograph craze, and of these requests I receive, I think, more than my share. But what is most surprising is the number of manuscripts I receive from young, aspiring authors. I am often asked " to read them, revise them carefully, and express an opinion as to the merit of the contribution." Why, I have frequently been requested to do a whole month's work on a single manuscript. What do I do with these? Well, the best I can. If I have a spare moment, I look over the story or article, and encourage the writer, if possible. But at times the supply is too great for physical endurance.'

" ' What exercise do you most indulge in, and what particular one do you recommend? '

" ' So far as I am concerned, I like a good, long walk, and this is what I would recommend to all who work with the brain and are confined. Exercise should never, in my opinion, be taken before sitting down to work, always after the task of the day has been completed. Then one receives far more benefit from it than if taken before work. I also like to work in my garden, and there is hardly a better means of exercise. Hunting and fishing are also favorite sports with me, and I keep a good gun and a fishing-rod close at hand.'

" ' Have you entirely given up gardening for literature? '

" ' Yes, almost entirely, even in an amateur way.

Of course I still retain an active interest in everything that is interesting or new about a garden or
a farm. But as to any active participation, as
formerly, I have been obliged to desist.'

"It may be interesting here to mention that the
grounds surrounding Mr. Roe's rural retreat at
Cornwall-on-the-Hudson show no lack of proper
care and attention. The property consists of
twenty-three acres and is all cultivated for floral
and farming purposes. The novelist has on these
grounds alone over one hundred and twelve different varieties of grapes, and has had in his strawberry
beds seventy different varieties of that luscious
berry in bearing at one time. One year Mr. Roe's
orchards yielded him, among other products, one
hundred and fifty barrels of apples, and this year
about forty bushels of pears will be taken from his
trees.

"'What are your immediate plans?' was asked
the novelist, as he courteously showed the writer
into the dining-room in response to the merry
jingle of the dinner-bell.

"'I am now taking a brief holiday, resting from
overwork. In about two months I leave the North
for Santa Barbara, California, where I may remain
for a year, or may return next spring. All depends
upon how my family and myself like the country
there. I go there partly for pleasure and partly

for work. I shall doubtless gather considerable new material, and this I shall incorporate in future works. I shall study the life of the people of that region, and intend more especially to devote myself to studying nature in the direction of trees, plants, as well as the animals, birds, etc., of that charming country. My return North is uncertain, as I have said, and should everything prove agreeable, I may extend my residence there indefinitely.'

"And here ended the writer's chat with perhaps the most popular author of the day. Mr. Roe is extremely retiring in disposition; he never courts notoriety, but always strictly avoids it whenever possible. And with his large black slouched hat set carelessly on his head a stranger would more readily mistake him for a Cuban planter, with his dark complexion, than the author of the novels which have entered into thousands of American homes."

"Cornwall is situated on the western bank of the Hudson, just north of the Highlands. If you arrive by steamer you find an energetic crowd of 'bus men, who are eager to be of service to you. Most of the vehicles have four horses attached, which seem to tell of a hill in the neighborhood. We passed Cornwall several times by boat, and saw enough of the energy of the hackmen to make us resolve to reach the place some time when they were absent. Consequently we sailed down on Cornwall as General Wolfe sailed down on Quebec — in a small boat, and captured the place easily.

" As we walked up the rickety steps that lead from the water to the wharf, there was no deputation there to meet us.

" ' Now the first thing,' said my companion, ' is to find out where Mr. Roe lives.'

" ' No, that 's the second thing,' I replied. ' The first thing is to find out where we are to get supper.'

" The reasonableness of this proposal was so apparent that further remark was not so necessary as finding a hotel well stocked with provisions.

" We found it in the shape of an unpretentious brick structure at the foot of the hill. By the way, everything is at the foot of the hill at Cornwall Landing. The landlady, who was the pink of neatness, promised us all we could eat on our return, although if she had known my talents in that line she would have hesitated. I noticed that she referred to ' Mr. Roe, the author,' while our fellow voyager in the small boat spoke of him as ' the strawberry man.' Probably the boor who relished the production of Mr. Roe's garden would have been surprised to know that the productions of his pen were even more sought after than that delicious fruit.

" But evening is coming on and we have a long hill before us, so we must proceed. A Cornwall road is always either going up or down, and a person gets great opportunities for rising in the world as he turns his back on the Hudson and climbs to Cornwall. The road winds up the hill, often shaded by trees and always accompanied by a mountain torrent whose rocky bed lies deep beside the pathway. This stream lacks only one thing to make it a success — and that is water. No doubt after a heavy rain it would show commendable enterprise, but now the rocks were dry. A thin thread of clear spring water trickled along the bottom of the ravine, now forming a silvery-toned waterfall, then losing itself among the loose rocks, next finding itself again, and sometimes making the mistake which humanity often makes, of spreading itself too much and trying to put on the airs of larger streams.

" Half-way up is a spring, surrounded by benches, welcome to the pedestrian who finds tramping up-hill business. The clear, cold water pours out, and an iron dipper, like Prometheus ' chained to a pillar,' invites the thirsty to have a drink. The benches form a semicircle around this fountain, and on the backs thereof some one has painted in large letters the legend 'Please don't cut an old friend.' But 'excelsior' is our motto, and we climb. When we reach the top of the mountain we part company with the rivulet, thinking, with perhaps a sigh, what a vast advantage water has over people — it always goes down hill. Cornwall now begins to show its beauties. It seems to be a big village composed of splendid residences and elegant family hotels — or rather huge summer boarding-houses. Excellent roads run in all directions, up and down, turning now to the right and now to the left, until a stranger loses all idea of the points of the compass.

"About a mile from the landing, if you are in a carriage, or about five miles if you are on foot, you come to an open gateway, through which a road turns that might be mistaken for one of the many offshoots of the public street, were it not that a notice conspicuously posted up informs the traveller that the way is private property. A cottage, probably a gardener's residence, stands beside the gate. The land slopes gently downward from the road and then rises beyond, leaving a wide valley between the street and a large two-story frame building that stands on the rising ground. This is the home of E. P. Roe, author of 'Barriers Burned Away,' 'Opening of a Chestnut Burr,' 'From Jest to Earnest,' and other well-known

10

works, read and enjoyed by thousands in America and in England.   Between the house and the road are long rows of strawberry plants that looked tempting even in September.   The house stands in about the centre of a plot of twenty-three acres. The side is toward the road, and a broad piazza runs along the length of it, from which glimpses of the distant Hudson can be had through the framework of trees and hills.   The piazza is reached by broad steps, and is high enough from the ground to make a grand tumbling-off place for the numerous jovial and robust youngsters that romp around there and call Mr. Roe 'papa.'   A wide hall runs through the centre of the house, and the whole dwelling has a roomy air that reminds one of the generous and hospitable mansions for which the South is famous.   Mr. Roe's house is without any attempt at architectural ornamentation, unless the roof window in the centre can be called an ornament; but there is something very homelike about the place, something that is far beyond the powers of architecture to supply.

" My fellow-traveller sat down in one of the rural chairs that stood invitingly on the piazza, and I manipulated the door-bell.

" While the servant is coming to open the door I may as well confess that I have undertaken to write the play of Hamlet with Hamlet left out.

" Mr. Roe was not at home.

" I tell this now so that the reader will not be disappointed when the girl opens the door.

" The door opens.

" Could we see Mr. Roe?

" Mr. Roe had left that very morning for New York.

" ' He evidently heard in some way we were coming,' said my companion, *sotto voce*.

" When would he return?

" Perhaps not this week. Would we walk in and see Mrs. Roe?

" The next thing to seeing an author is to see the author's wife, so we accepted the invitation and walked into the parlor. Before we walked out we came to the conclusion that the next thing to seeing the author's wife is to see the author.

" Now, of course, I might have taken an inventory of the articles in the parlor, just as if I were a deputy sheriff, or a tax collector, or something of that sort, but I did n't. I might tell of the piano that stood in one corner and the pile of music that reached from the floor to the top of it, and of the little table covered with stereoscopic views, and the photograph of Mr. Roe framed above it, and of the two low front windows with their river view and their lace curtains, and the large folding-doors opening into the library, the workshop of Mr. Roe, and of the quiet, neutral tints of the carpet, or the many contents of the whatnot in the corner, and the paintings and engravings on the walls, and the comfortable easy-chairs, and the books scattered here and there, and of dozens of other things that made up an author's parlor, but I will not mention one of them.

"I had the idea that E. P. Roe was a kindly old gentleman with gray hair. Kindly he undoubtedly is, but old he is not. His portrait shows him to have a frank, manly countenance, with an earnest and somewhat sad expression. He has dark hair and a full beard, long and black. Mr. Roe is at present writing a series of articles on small fruits for *Scribner's Magazine*. The publishers of that periodical intend to give a portrait of Mr. Roe, which will be the first ever published. It may appear in the December number, and if it does the readers of this paper are respectfully referred to the pages of that magazine. It seems to be the general idea that Mr. Roe is an old man. For instance, a lady writing from Wheeling, W. Va., to *The Household* a few weeks since, says : —

"'Some one asked if Rev. E. P. Roe had taken his characters from life or not. Several years ago we had amongst us a certain Professor Roe (vocal teacher, possessing a beautiful tenor voice), said to be a son of the novelist. If he was a son, the character of Walter

Gregory in " Opening of a Chestnut Burr " was certainly drawn from him, and it always seemed to me that Dennis Fleet's wonderful voice in " Barriers Burned Away " was likened to his voice.'

" If this writer could have seen the youthful appearance of Mrs. Roe, she would have no hesitation in denying the professor's alleged relationship to the novelist. Her husband is not yet forty.

"I wish Scribners would publish a portrait of Mrs. Roe. It would certainly add to the popularity of the magazine. Such a lady must be a wonderful help to her husband. I think, as a general thing, the world gives too little credit to the power behind the throne.

"Mrs. Roe deserves at least half the credit of 'Barriers Burned Away,' which is certainly E. P. Roe's most dramatic work, and had, no doubt, a great deal to do with many of his other volumes. This particular work describes the thrilling scenes of the Chicago fire with a vividness and power that is rarely surpassed. When the whole world was thrilled by the dreadful tidings of a city's destruction, Mr. Roe said to his wife that if he could collect some of the actual occurrences that must be transpiring there he thought he could write a book about it. Mrs. Roe at once decided for him. Her advice was that so tersely put by Mr. Greeley. Although nearly a thousand miles intervened, Mr. Roe was in Chicago before the fire had ceased, and the incidents so graphically depicted in 'Barriers Burned Away' were the result of actual observation.

"Most of Mr. Roe's characters are taken from real life, and all of his works are written for a purpose, as can readily be seen in 'What Can She Do?' for example. His next book, which will be published in a few days, will furnish another instance of writing for a purpose. Its title is, 'Without a Home;' the subject it treats is the tenement-house problem, which is at present agitating New York and all large cities. In this work the scenes and personages will be nearly all from real life. If the book were not in press the tenement-house fires in New York on Friday, causing the death of seven persons, would furnish a tragic climax to his story. What could be more terribly pathetic than the frantic mother penned in by the smoke and flame, dragging herself to the bedside of her children to die with them? In choosing the evils of the tenement-house system as a subject, Mr. Roe strikes at one of the worst features of city life.

"It was to finish the last pages of this book that Mr. Roe was now 'Without a Home' himself, and as the printers were clamoring for copy, he had betaken himself to a room in a New York hotel to write without interruption.   Mr. Roe is too good-natured to deny himself to visitors, and they make great inroads on his time.

" ' If he hears the voice of a friend,' said Mrs. Roe, ' he cannot remain at his desk.'

" So when there is work that must be done, Mr. Roe banishes himself from home and friends and flies to that loneliness which only a great and crowded city can supply.

" Mrs. Roe's favorite book is ' The Opening of a Chestnut Burr,' and this must be a favorite work with many, for it has reached its thirtieth thousand, not to mention the numerous reprints in England and Canada.   The realistic incident in this work, which supplies the place the Chicago fire does in the other, is the sinking in mid ocean of the French steamer Ville d'Havre.

" I think, although it is only mere conjecture on my part, that Mrs. Roe herself is the heroine of this book.   For that reason I shall not attempt to say anything of the lady, as the reader can turn to the book and satisfy all curiosity there.   But if I should find, at some future time, that I am mistaken in my surmise, I shall make that my excuse for the pleasant task of writing again of Mrs. Roe. The old homestead is described in the ' Opening of a Chestnut Burr,' and naturally this would endear the book to those who lived there.

" The library in which Mr. Roe does his writing, when at home, is a sunny room filled from floor to ceiling with books. A large flat desk, covered with papers, stands in the centre of the room, and this is the novelist's work-bench. I shall conclude with a few words regarding Mr. Roe's method of working. Mr. Roe himself has supplied this in a letter written nearly a year ago, to an admirer, and part of which I am allowed to copy. This extract forms a portion of Mr. Roe's work never before published, and the writer himself had no idea it would ever appear in print. The letter bears date November 25, 1878. He says: —

" ' My aim is to spend the earlier part of the day in my study, but I cannot always control my time, much of which is lost in interruptions. I sometimes have to go away and shut myself up for a time. I am not as systematic as I ought to be. I like to write the latter part of my books at white heat, first getting full of my story and then writing with a zest. I call from five to eight pages a good day's work, although in some moods I write many more. Again, I will work hard over three or four. I am opposed to night work.

" ' I hope to average five hours a day hereafter in my study, and three or four in my garden. I employ from ten to fifteen men and from ten to thirty boys in picking the berries. A large part

THE STUDY AT " ROELANDS."

of my labor is employed in taking up and packing plants. The department of fruit culture to which I give my chief attention, is the keeping of each variety separate and pure. This I trust to no one, and it requires constant vigilance.'

"After leaving the residence of Mr. Roe, we went half a mile or so farther on to Idlewild, once the home of N. P. Willis. Darkness came on before we reached there and we had our labor for our pains.

"Mrs. Roe said that Idlewild is little changed since the poet left it. A recent freshet swept away the bridges he built in the Glen, but otherwise it is the same as it was before. Thus ended our visit to Cornwall-on-the-Hudson."

CHAPTER XI

SANTA BARBARA

MY brother's boyhood friend, Mr. Merwin, speaking of his visits at Cornwall later, says: "When honors came in troops, I found Edward was the same kindly unostentatious man, the truly loyal friend. Later, after some correspondence with me, he came to Southern California, where under those sunny skies and semi-tropical scenes his love of Nature found great delight.

"While visiting at Pasadena, as we drove about that beautiful city, he emphasized what he had often told me, that one of the great joys of his life was that which came to him from the hundreds of letters from all parts of the country, and many written by people in humble circumstances, thanking him most heartily for the cheer and encouragement he had given them through his books."

After a short stay with his friend in Pasadena Edward went with his wife and children to Santa Barbara. There they occupied a pleasantly situated cottage, owned by a New England lady and her daughter, under whose excellent care they enjoyed the rest and freedom from restraint that cannot be found in crowded hotels.

In a letter written to the Detroit *Tribune* my brother gives his experience of a California winter.

" My impression is that January first was the warmest day of the month. Certainly on no other days was I so conscious of the sun's heat, yet the air was so deliciously cool and fresh in the early morning. There had been a heavy dew, and grass, weed, hedge, and flower were gemmed in the brilliant sunshine.

" Walking up town with my mail at about ten in the morning, I found myself perspiring as upon a hot day in August, but there was no sense of oppression. One was exhilarated rather than wilted. After reaching our cottage piazza and the shelter of the climbing roses and honeysuckle, the change was decidedly marked. This is said to be the peculiarity the year round, even in midsummer. One has only to step out of the sun's rays in order to be cool, and the dead, sultry heat which sometimes induces one to yearn for the depths of a cave is unknown.

" As I sat there in the shade, letting the paper fall from my hand in the deeper interest excited by my immediate surroundings, I could scarcely realize that we were in the depths of winter.

"The air was fragrant from blooming flowers; finches and Audubon's warblers were full of song in the pepper trees, while humming birds were almost as plentiful as bumble-bees in June.

"It was evident that the day was being celebrated in the manner characteristic of the place. One might fancy that half the population were on horseback. In twos and fours they clattered along the adjacent streets, while from more distant thoroughfares, until the sounds were like faint echoes, came also the sounds of horses' feet rapidly striking the hard adobe of the roadways. In addition to those who gave the impression of life and movement in the suburbs of the town, large equestrian parties had started for mountain passes and distant cañons, taking with them hearty lunches in which the strawberries were a leading feature. As long as the sun was well above the horizon delicate girls, almost in summer costume, could sit in the shade of the live-oaks in safety, but when the sun declines to a certain point, between four and five in winter, there is a sudden chill in the air, and those who do not protect themselves by wraps or overcoats are likely to be punished with as severe colds as they would take in a Boston east wind.

"It has often seemed to me warmer at eight o'clock in the evening than at four in the afternoon.

"We resolved to have our holiday outing as well as the others, and after dinner were bowling out on the road to Montecito, the favorite suburb of Santa Barbara. The fields by the roadside were as bare and brown as ours in winter when not covered with snow, but drought, not frost, was the cause. The 'rainy season' was well advanced, but there had been no rain in quantity sufficient to awaken nature from her sleep. In this climate vegetation is always a question of moisture.

"When reaching the villa region of Montecito, blossoming gardens and green lawns illustrated this truth. After a visit to the beautiful grounds and fine residence of Mr. A. L. Anderson, so well remembered by thousands as the captain of the favorite Hudson River steamboat the Mary Powell, we drove on to one of the largest orange groves on this part of the coast. Mr. Johnson, one of the proprietors, received us most hospitably, and led the way into a grove that sloped toward the mountains. The ground was scrupulously free from weeds, mellow as an ash heap, and had evidently been made very fertile. Mr. Johnson told me that he fed the trees constantly and liberally, and this course is in accordance with nature and with reason, for the orange tree never rests. While the fruit is ripening the tree is blossoming for a new crop. Always growing and producing, it requires a constant supply of plant food, and one of the causes of the deep green and vigorous aspect of the grove and its fruitfulness consisted undoubtedly in the richness at the roots.

"Another and leading cause was in abundant supply of water.

"From a cañon near by a mountain stream flowed down skirting the grove. This stream was tapped by an iron pipe at a point sufficiently high to furnish by gravity all the water required, and it was distributed by a simple yet ingenious contrivance.

"The utmost vigilance is exercised against insect pests and the mutilation of the roots by gophers. The results of all this intelligent care and cultivation were seen in the surprising beauty and fruitfulness of the trees, which were laden with from one to two thousand golden-hued oranges, in addition to the green ones not to be distinguished from the leaves at a distance. Even so early in the season there were a sufficient number of blossoms to fill the air with fragrance.

"The brook babbled with a summer-like sound, and the illusion of summer was increased by the song of birds, the flutter of butterflies, and the warm sunshine, rendering vivid the gold and glossy green of the groves. Rising near and reflecting down the needed heat were the rocky and precipitous slopes of the Santa Ynez Mountains. Turning on one's heel, the silver sheen of the Pacific Ocean, gemmed with islands, stretched away as far as the eye could reach. Could this be January? On our way home I felt that it might be, for as the sun sank low wraps and overcoats, which could not have been endured an hour before, seemed scarcely adequate protection against the sudden chill.

"Throughout the month there were many days like the first, summer — like sunshine followed by chilly evenings and cool nights. No rain fell and clouds were rarely seen. The temperature gradually became lower even at midday, and occasionally in the early morning there was a white frost on the boards and sidewalks. The roses grew more scattering in the bushes. Nature did not absolutely stop and rest, but she went slow over the cold divide of the year. I know not how it was with the old residents, but a sense of winter haunted me, especially on the quiet, star-lit nights. I sometimes questioned whether this sense resulted from the impressions of a lifetime, made at this season, or was due to climatic influences. To both, I fancy. When a baker's horse and wagon, furnished with bells, jingled by, it was a sleigh until memory asserted itself.

"When abroad, even in the bright, warm sunshine, something in the appearance of the sky, the feel of the atmosphere, and the aspect of the bare, brown fields suggested winter and created a momentary astonishment at the flowers which continued to bloom in the watered gardens.

"I was continually aware of a conscious effort to account for what I saw and to readjust my ideas to a new order of things.

"The season seemed an anomaly, for it was neither summer nor winter, fall nor spring, in accordance with one's previous impressions. The visage of nature had an odd and peculiar aspect. It was as if the face of an old friend had assumed an expression never seen before. There was no ambiguity or uncertainty upon one point, however, and that was the need of winter clothing by day and of blankets at night, roses and sunshine notwithstanding, and those proposing to come here should always remember the chill of shade and apartments without fires.

"Although the mercury never marks extreme cold, the sense of cold is often felt keenly unless adequate provision is made against it. All that is needed, however, is a little prudence, for one never has to guard against sudden and violent changes.

"As in the East, so here, winter is especially dedicated to social pleasures. Much of the gayety centres at the two fine hotels, the Arlington and the San Marcos, both under the efficient management of one proprietor, Mr. Cowles. The townspeople are much indebted to his genial courtesy, and the spacious parlours are often lined with the parents and chaperons of young ladies from the city of Santa Barbara as well as with his guests, while the entertainments have the best characteristics of a dancing party at a private dwelling. It is very fortunate for the young people that there are such unexceptional places in which to meet, for this town is peculiarly a city of cottages, few being large enough for assemblies of any considerable numbers.

"There is consequently much social life in a quiet, informal way.

"One of the remarkable characteristics of the town is the large percentage of what is justly termed good society — a society not resting its claims on wealth or an ancestry long known and recognised in the vicinity, but on the much better qualities of refinement, intelligence, and cultivation. Search for health and a genial climate have brought people here from all parts of the Union, and not a few, after long residence abroad, prefer this Pacific slope to any of the world-renowned regions on the Mediterranean. One therefore

soon discovers a marked absence of provincialism
and is led to expect that the quiet lady or gentleman to whom he is introduced has seen far more
of the world than himself.   The small, unpretentious cottage facing the grassy sidewalk may be
inhabited by a mechanic, or it may be the dwell-
ing-place of people cosmopolitan in their culture
and experience.   Strangers are not wholly dependent on each other for society, as is so often
true of health resorts, but find a resident population both hospitable and acquainted with life in its
most varied aspects.   Much of the abundant leisure possessed by many is spent in reading, and to
this pleasure a large, well-selected free library
contributes greatly."

Edward had the good fortune to arrive at Santa
Barbara in time to witness its unique centennial celebration, of which he gives a detailed
description.

"Santa Barbara, Cal., January 7, 1887.

"Few more interesting events ever took place
in the quaint and quiet town of Santa Barbara
than its centennial, and nothing resembling it in
any true sense can ever occur again.   The Indian
element of this region receded and disappeared
before the Spanish, and the latter population is
fast becoming a minority among the still paler

faces arriving from the East. The time perhaps is not distant when Santa Barbara may be known as a New England city. Even in its centennial the great effort made to recall the past and the old resulted in a large degree from the interest taken by new comers in vanishing phases of life. The success of the enterprise was due largely to the organization, young in age and composed chiefly of youthful members, entitled the 'Go Ahead Club.' The name itself suggests the East, and the opposite of the Spanish disposition to permit each day to be a repetition of a former day, yet the club had the tact and friendly feeling to co-operate with the best Spanish element, and to bring about a festival week which interested all classes of people.

"For days even a stranger was impressed by a slight bustle of preparation. When riding up from the steamer we saw, in the dim starlight, that a great arch spanned Main Street. Observation in the bright sunshine of the morrow proved this arch to be a wooden structure and a fine imitation of the front of the old mission with its quaint towers. Busy workmen were draping the edifice with some variety of aromatic evergreen and with palm leaves, and it still remains as a suggestion to new comers of what they missed in not arriving earlier.

"The opening ceremonies of the week naturally centered at the Mission Church, and on Sunday the religious phase of the festival culminated. Even before we were through breakfast groups were seen pressing from town. Later there were the sounds of rapid wheels and the echoing tramp of horses. We soon joined the increasing throng wending its way up the slopes which lift the Mission above the town and place it against the grand mountain background. Spanish colors, red and yellow, hung from tower to tower, while American flags floated from the belfry arches. Within the long, narrow interior of the church the sunshine contended with innumerable candles flickering on the altar, at the shrines, and from the chandeliers. The softly blended light revealed the beautiful decorations drawn from the abundant flora and plant life of the region.

"The elaborate service began, the fragrance of roses was lost in that of the incense, the rustle of dresses and tread of incoming feet in the mellow tones of the chanting priest and the responses of the choir. Every seat and all standing room was occupied, rich and poor sharing alike according to the earliness of their arrival. Next to a dark-visaged Spanish laborer might be seen the delicate bloom of a New England girl's features. Beautiful lace mantillas were worn in several instances. In looking at them one sighed as he thought of the various monstrosities termed bonnets which disfigure modern women. The clergy were in their most gorgeous robes, strong contrasts in tone and color on every side, but above all was a sense of the past touching the present in many and unexpected ways; and this effect was enhanced by a sermon in English, giving an account of the founding of the Mission. Late one afternoon, on a subsequent day, I found the door of the church open and, venturing in, saw the western sun shining through the high narrow windows, lighting up shrines and images with the mellowest light and throwing others into the deepest shadow.

"No one was visible, yet in the silence and desertion of the place one felt more like worship than when, a part of the throng, he witnessed the ceremonials of the preceding Sunday.

"Later still, returning from a ramble in Mission Cañon, I peeped into the old church once more. Twilight had deepened into dusk — all was dark within, except the faintest glimmer of a taper at the altar, where it was evident that some of the Franciscans were engaged in their devotions. As I crept noiselessly away the bells chimed out from the belfry. In the upper gallery of the long corridor stretching from the right of the chapel there was an immediate opening of doors and a shuffling of feet.

"Evidently the bells had summoned to some new duty, — attendance in the refectory at that hour, I trust, — and I could have cordially joined the venerable fathers then, however simple their diet.

"On Monday the festival passed into its secular aspect. The morning was deemed most unfavorable in this climate, where a cloud, even in winter, is far more rare than roses. The sky was overcast with what the Spaniards call a 'high fog.' The sun soon proved, however, to be the victor, for early in the day the leaden pall was shot through and through with light. Not only from the most distant and well-to-do ranches, but from all the small adobe houses and huts that skirt the mountains, the people were on the way to town in the early hours. They appeared on the streets in almost every description of vehicle imaginable, and not a few looked as if they had trudged from a long distance. The majority, both of men and women, had apparently ridden in on their broncho horses, the hardy and often vicious native breed of the region. The townspeople had prepared a brilliant welcome, for the whole length of State Street was decorated with flags and streamers of many and varied

devices, the Spanish and American colors blending most amicably. There was bustle and movement, life and color, with an increasing concourse
throughout the whole length of the thoroughfare.
To a stranger's eye, men in various costumes
were riding aimlessly and often furiously to and
fro, but as noon approached affairs began to cul-
minate in the blocks above the Arlington Hotel.
Here the procession was forming, and it proved
to be the chief event of the week. Nature was
now assisting to make the occasion all that could
be desired. The clouds that had threatened now
merely saved the day from an unredeemed glare.
After the usual delay in processions, it began
to pass the balcony of the Arlington Hotel, where
scores of guests were assembled to witness the
pageant. First came the grand marshal in a genuine Mexican suit and mantle. Following him
were his aids, dressed in rich, various, and characteristic Spanish costumes, some of which were
remarkable for their beauty and others were picturesque in the extreme. One young gentleman
was habited in blue, lavishly laced with silver.
It was the cadet uniform of the Spanish army, and
had belonged to his grandfather. Another, clad
in cream white satin and gold lace, with crimson
sash and other accessories, made a striking figure.

"Indeed, each of the aides graced the occasion

in handsome costumes which were, as I was told, no capricious and fancy affairs, but a reproduction of the gala habiliments of the past. They sat their fine horses in Mexican saddles which were in themselves marvels of old and curious workmanship. A like cavalcade in Broadway would draw out the town.

"Next in order came the Spanish division, men and women on horseback, and nearly fifty strong. It was evident that all heirlooms in dress had been rummaged from their receptacles and made to fit the descendants of remote ancestors. It would be hard to say how many different ages and how many provinces in Spain and Mexico were represented.

"To modern eyes the picturesque had the ascendency over other qualities, but all welcomed the man carrying a guitar. At any rate, this division passed all too quickly, singing an ancient Spanish song. Close upon them were a band of soldiers clad in suits of antiquated buff jerkins, armed in old Mexican style with long pikes and muskets that may have been formidable once. It is doubtful whether a band so representative of the old Spanish element will ever appear on the streets of an American town again. Years hence such an attempt will be more of a masquerade than a reproduction. In this instance the genuine

Spaniards were too numerous and their traditions too recent and real to permit impositions.

"Many Spaniards and native Californians not in costume now followed, and then came an old-fashioned ox-cart, dating back a century and drawn by oxen yoked by the horns. Within the cart was a wooden plow that had turned some of the earliest furrows in this region, and would have been equally satisfactory at the time of Abraham. In this age of invention one wonders that people remained satisfied so long with such primitive methods and implements. Appropriately following the cart, the like of which had been used by their ancestors, came the shrunken band of Mission Indians, the two foremost of them carrying a portrait, draped in Spanish colors, of Padre Junupero Serra.

"The good father passed away centuries ago, and the Indians he sought to civilize are also nearly extinct, but the principles which actuated him have redeemed his name from forgetfulness and will crown it with increasing honor.

"The half-dozen Indians were chanting some wild song of their own when the fine band from San Luis Obispo struck up and the wail-like echo of the past was lost. Then came another significant and diminishing company, the Grand Army of the Republic. On every public occasion the ranks are thinner and the hair of the veterans grayer. They, too, will soon leave but a name, but it will not be forgotten.

"Driving away sad, if not gloomy thoughts, comes now a vision of beauty and youth; the joy of to-day and the rich promise of the future — an indefinite number of young girls who, in their two-wheeled village carts, or 'tubs,' as the English term them, drew forth rapturous applause. Well they might, for they were in harmony with the loveliness of the June-like day. Their little carts had been transformed into floral bowers. The flowers and greenery so festooned the horses that they were half-hidden, while wheels within wheels of smilax, roses, geraniums, daisies, and other blossoms revolved in unison with the outer circumferences. Each little cart had its own distinctive character, and some had been decorated with rare taste and originality. Not a few of the girls carried parasols constructed entirely of roses, or of geraniums, passion flowers, orange blossoms, etc. Greenhouses had not been stripped for them, nor, indeed, the open gardens from which they had been taken. Truly, no such visible and delightful proof could have been given to our Northern eyes that we had come to the land of flowers. Gardens, orange trees golden with fruit, formed the background for this charming part of the procession, while beyond and above all rose the grand Santa Ynez Mountains, softening their rugged outlines with half-veiling mists.

"Burlesque followed close upon beauty in the form of an old farm cart laden with the coarser vegetables and driven by two young men in the garb of ancient females. The trades' procession came next, and spoke well for the business of the city, but our eyes soon dwelt lovingly on over a hundred school children, who made, by their unrestrained laughter, the sweetest music of the day, while two little girls riding on one much-bedecked donkey caused ripples of merriment as they passed.

"A cavalcade of carriages and of ladies and gentlemen on horseback seemed about to close the procession, when there appeared one of the most interesting features yet seen — a train of pack mules, not merely illustrating the former method of transportation, but that employed to-day by the owner of the train. I hastened to the director, whose dress indicated a rude mountaineer, and expected a half intelligible reply from a Spaniard. The accent of his first word led me to scan his delicate Anglo-Saxon features. I eventually learned that he was a New Yorker, a member of one of its best-known families, and not a native of a little-known wilderness.

"Nevertheless he is a mountaineer. Dressed for a Fifth Avenue company one would not suspect it, his form is so slight and complexion so fair. Dudes would not be abashed at his presence, yet they would expire under one day of his experiences.

"Only by a mule train, led over a scarcely practicable trail, can he reach his distant ranch, that is forty-five miles back in the heart of the mountains. Here, with another young man, a kindred spirit, he cares for an increasing herd of cattle, and if necessary is ready to protect it from wild animals. The grazing grounds are far within a region about as wild as it ever has been. How about the young men who whine when they can find nothing to do?

"The interest of the two closing days of the festival centered at the race course and at the pavilion. The chief attractions at the former place were to be seen on Tuesday, and they were of a mixed character. We were treated to what would seem to be a rather rare phenomenon in Santa Barbara — a genuine Indian summer day of the warmest type, as we know it at the East. A haze partly obscured the Santa Ynez Mountains, softened the outlines of the foothills and blended the ocean with the sky. The air was soft and balmy in the extreme, but one soon detected a slight chill in the shade. All sorts of vehicles, from stages of unwieldy height, open barouches, farmers' wagons of all descriptions, top buggies, down to the numerous little two-wheeled carts, rapidly converged toward the judges' stand. As on all gala occasions here, however, the number on horseback was very large, the ladies sitting their horses with perfect ease and grace. Not a few, like myself, were content to trudge to the rendezvous on foot. The grand stand was soon crowded, and the vast, restless concourse stretched far to the right and left on either side of the race track. The horsemanship of the Spaniards could only be surpassed by the fine action of their steeds, and all lovers of this noblest of animals must have been delighted. In the effort to show how wild cattle were lassoed, thrown, and branded there appeared to be too much needless cruelty, and when a miserable little bull was tormented into savageness, and the semblance of a bull-fight took place, scores of people turned away in disgust.

"The finest equestrianism could not redeem the scene from brutality. The victims were the wretched bull, a fine innocent horse badly gored, and the people who could not endure to see animals suffer needlessly. So also in the afternoon great skill was undoubtedly manifested in

lassoing the feet of the wild broncho horses, and
in the process of subduing them, yet one pitied
the poor creatures too greatly for enjoyment and
soon turned away. The helpless beasts were
checked in full career, often thrown upon their
heads, turning a complete somersault. One
animal, I was told, broke its neck in the opera-
tion, and so escaped further suffering. Such
scenes, no doubt, illustrated much that was common in the life of the early settlers, but happily
it is a past phase, and will scarcely be reproduced
again in this region.

"It was interesting to observe the many types
of people in festival costume, the Indian in his
blanket, the Spaniard wearing the broad som-
brero, and the belle from New York reflecting
the latest mode. There was movement, light,
color, vivacity, and excitement.

"Every moment or two the eye caught glimpses
of swift, spirited horses and their graceful riders,
and yet one's glance was often lured from it all
to the grand, mist-veiled mountains beyond.
Many of the scenes and objects at the pavilion
were very interesting to our foreign eyes and
ears. Here Spanish and American life met and
mingled in a far more agreeable way. Several
ladies had taken charge of the large building,
erected for horticultural purposes, and by the aid

of greenery, flowers, flags, and a blending of Spanish and American colors, had transformed the
spacious interior into a decorated hall well fitted
for a festival. In the centre of the hall rose a
flower stand suggesting Moorish architecture, its
arches making fitting frames for the young girls
within. One might buy flowers, but his eye
lingered rather on the fair flower-girls in their
charming costumes. Among the booths was one
in which some Spanish ladies had kindly permitted to be exhibited some of their ancient treas-
ures — velvet mantles, embroidered shawls, etc.
Even to masculine eyes they were marvellously
beautiful, rich, and intricate in their designs.
The ladies stood before them with clasped hands
and expressed themselves in exclamation points.
The chief attraction, however, was the stage, on
which were tableaux and, above all, the genuine
Spanish fandango. One of the dances was a
waltz, with an intricate figure which you felt
might go on forever, and that you could look on
a good part of the time. At first it struck one
as merely simple, graceful, and very slow, and
guided by monotonous music; but while you
looked and listened a fascination grew upon you
hard to account for. The oft-repeated strain
began to repeat itself in your mind; you felt
rather than saw how it controlled the leisurely

gliding figures — for there is no hopping in the Spanish dances — until at last, in fancy, you were moving with them in perfect time and step. In brief, the dance had the effect of a strain of music which, when first heard, is not at all striking, yet is soon running in your head as if it had a spell not easily broken. On the programme the dance was entitled 'Contra Danza.' Later a Spaniard who has a wide local reputation, I believe, appeared in what was termed 'Son-jarabe.' He certainly left nothing to be desired in his performance after his fashion, but the grace of the lady who accompanied was inimitable. From my somewhat distant point of view she appeared to be dressed in a simple black gown and wore no ornaments. She needed none. No bespangled dancer I ever saw so enchained my eyes. One would almost think that an orange, placed upon her head, would not fall off, and yet a more utter absence of stiffness in movement was never witnessed. She seemed ever approaching, yet ever receding from, her companion; a moment near, then far away, gliding to one side or the other, as if impossible to be reached in her coquetry of elusive grace. Each separate movement was called out in Spanish, and in a varied, half-musical accent not easily described.

"At the closing centennial ball like dances were

repeated, the participants wearing Spanish costumes. Here we had a nearer and more distinct view of the fandango. We again saw the 'Contra Danza,' and another, even more intricate, that was as odd as it was full of grace and unexpected action. If 'La Jota' is an old dance, it should certainly take the place of many that have little to redeem them from commonplace, if not worse.

"Son-jarabe was again repeated to the pleasure of all, and especially of the Spaniards, who, in conformance with an old custom, expressed their satisfaction by raining silver down upon the floor from the gallery. There was the same weird intoning by the master of ceremonies, calling off the different measures; the same constantly recurring strains of music that haunted one long afterward, and the same slow yet singularly graceful movement of the dancers. All were in Spanish costume, although many American young men and maidens were also participants, yet had been taught so well by their Spanish friends that they were scarcely to be distinguished from them. The Spanish dances that I saw did not strike me as at all voluptuous, and no one appeared who was not dressed in accordance with the strictest ideas of decorum. The whole pageant passed away with the ball, and nothing remains to remind us of the centennial but the green arch spanning State Street. The old Mission stands out gray and silent, except that its bells occasionally chime out for reasons unknown to me."

Writing again, in April, my brother describes the change wrought by the first heavy rainfall of the season.

"One of the drawbacks to Santa Barbara is the dust, and it is a disagreeable accompaniment of a dry climate which must be accepted. Towards the end of January there were occasionally high, gusty winds which reminded one of March experiences at home. At times the dust rose in clouds and obscured the city, and to my taste the wildest snowstorm would be preferable to these chilling, stifling tempests. They were not frequent or long continued, however, and the old inhabitants said they presaged rain, the great bounty for which the whole State was longing.

"A rainless winter is a terrible misfortune, and when February finds the ground hard and dry there is deep and natural anxiety.

"In one dry season, years ago, forty thousand head of cattle perished. With present means of communication this probably would not happen again, but a check would be given to budding

prosperity which would take several fruitful years
to overcome. There were scores of people hesi-
tating whether to buy or build who would decide
favorably if the usual rainfall occurred. When,
therefore, on the 5th the first storm of the season
set in, rejoicing and congratulations were general.
Seldom before have I so realized what a heavenly bounty rain is. The whole population were
hoping, waiting, longing, and one would be callous
indeed not to sympathize. For that matter, the
interests of temporary visitors were also deeply
involved, as may be illustrated by the pleasure I
had in watching from my study window the bare,
brown foothills become greener daily. With
intervals, designed, it would seem, to give the
parched earth time to take in the precious moisture, the rains continued for about ten days. At
last there was a steady down-pour for nearly
twenty-four hours, and then dawned a morning
that for brightness, clearness, and beauty left
nothing to be imagined. The birds were fairly
ecstatic in their rejoicings and nature seemed to
be tripping forth like a young girl to her work.
It may be that she will have to perfect most of the
products of the earth without another drop of rain,
and she will prove equal to the task.

"A fruitful year in this section does not depend
on seasonable storms and showers, as with us, but

upon the number of inches of the winter rainfall, the soil retaining sufficient moisture to carry the crops through in safety. Many tourists came in the height of the storm and some had a hard time of it. The hotels were crowded, and not a few, miserably seasick, were driven from house to house in pouring rain searching for rooms. Except on State Street the highways of the city are little more than country roads, the bottom of which, as in Virginia, seems to have fallen out. One stage load was spilled into the mud and no doubt carried away sinister memories of "sunny Santa Barbara." The weather, which was the salvation of the country, was well anathematized by transient visitors, and one lady was overheard to remark that she had seen the first of the place and hoped that she had seen the last. Thus judgments and opinions are formed. Those who remained and saw the exquisite phases of spring rapidly developing under the vivid sunshine would be in no hurry to see the last of Santa Barbara, and a more perfect summer morning has rarely been seen than dawned on the last day of the month."

CHAPTER XIII

RETURN TO CORNWALL — LETTERS

I SPENT the summer of 1887 with Edward and his family at Santa Barbara; and he left me there in September on his return to his home at Cornwall. ·He expected to come back during the winter of 1889; and just a week before his sudden death, while I was at the Western Chautauqua, near Monterey, I had my last letter from him, telling of his plans for a California story which he hoped to write when once more at Santa Barbara.

That evening, Major-General O. O. Howard gave a lecture upon the Battle of Gettysburg, and at its close I had some conversation with him, in the course of which I spoke of the letter just received. He had been well acquainted with my brother at West Point. I remember his saying at this time: "I gave a copy of 'A Knight of the Nineteenth Century' to a young man about whose course of life I felt great anxiety, and that book, he wrote me, was the means of his entire reformation."

This is but one of many similar instances that came before me personally during my sojourn in the West.

At the time of Edward's departure from Santa Barbara he had engaged to write a story for *Harper's Magazine* which should be a sequel to "Nature's Serial," and which was to be fully illustrated by Mr. William Hamilton Gibson. It was therefore necessary for him to be near the scenes of his proposed story and in easy communication with Mr. Gibson.

It may not be out of place to print here the following letters. Many of them are separated by long intervals of time and have no direct connection with each other, but they are expressive of the warm friendship that existed between my brother and the talented artist.

"SANTA BARBARA, July 17, 1887.

"MY DEAR MR. GIBSON, — The longer I remain here and the more I see of this region the oftener I think of you: and the more earnestly I am bent on your coming here with your sketch-book.

"The scenery is just in your line, yet different from any thing you have yet done. Phew! what a book we could make together out here. During the past week Mrs. Roe and I went over the

Santa Ynez Mountains, and I wished for you at every turn of the San Marcus Pass.   Then there are scores of these, with beautiful cañons.   But I will tell you about them in September, when I hope to see you.

"I expect to give much of September and all of October to the study of the Highlands, and only wish you can so arrange as to be with me as much as possible.

"I've been toiling over the Earthquake story, and while you and the critics will say it is no great 'shakes,' I shall have to remember how the mountain labored.   I have at least a month's more work upon it, and am giving up the whole of my time to it, now that I am in the mood for writing.

"How are you enjoying the summer, and are you very busy?

"Lucky you did not get into that fight with the Park Commissioners during your July heats.   If you had there would have been some 'ha'r lifted,' as they say out on the plains.   You would make a better subject for a scalping-knife than I.   Have you seen much of Mr. Alden?   He sent me two fine photographs of himself recently.

"I trust that Mrs. Gibson and the boy are keeping well through the intense heat of which we read in the papers.   This climate surpasses anything I ever imagined. We have had but one hot day thus far. July has been delightfully cool, about the same as last December, with the exception that the evenings and nights are a little warmer. The sea-bathing is superb. Mrs. Roe and all five children are enjoying it this afternoon.

"Yours sincerely, E. P. ROE."

"WASHINGTON, Conn., September, 1887.

"Hurrah! Hurrah! Welcome home, one and all! Such is the burden of my emotions as I read in to-day's paper that Mr. Roe, the Roe-manser, has returned to civilization from the Santa Barbarans, and is once more at 'Shanty Clear.'

"Seriously, I am immensely delighted that you are once more with us, and shall look forward to an early meeting. And now apropos — we, my wife and I, have enjoyed many a memorable season of pleasure at your country home. Can we not persuade you and Mrs. Roe to give us a visit at ours? for here is my favorite camping ground and my home acre. As soon as you feel sufficiently rested from your trip, and providing you are so disposed, will you make us happy by spending a few days with us? — that is if you still remember your neglectful correspondent and care to hob-nob with him as of yore.

"That proposed Highland trip is immensely tempting, and I shall hope to arrange to take a few days outing with you, but alas! it cannot be until early November or the very last of October. I am so *full* of obligations until then.

"Don't call this a letter. It is written in the face of a yawning mail-bag and must be judged accordingly.

"Your sincere friend,

"GIBSON."

Mr. Gibson's own work was so pressing that autumn that he was unable to spare the time for the Highland trip mentioned in his letter, when many of the sketches were to be made for the projected story. The remaining letters are from my brother to Mr. Gibson.

"December 15, 1880.

"Some one rang at my door to-day — he must be nigh of kin to Santa Claus — and left your superb volume. It almost took away my breath.

"I gave you 'Small Fruits' only. But the fruits of your pencil and pen are the reverse of small.

"Do you realize what a benefactor you are in sending me, on this dull cloudy day, exquisites of the finest seasons of the year? Spring is months away, but I have had the sweetest glimpse of spring beside my winter fire.   The blazing wood supplied the warmth, — and your fancy did the rest in reproducing June.

"I am deeply in your debt.   Draw on me for unlimited quantities of strawberries."

"April 16, 1882.

"I was determined to find you a four-leaf clover, and yesterday I succeeded.

"It will bring you no end of good luck."

"January 31, 1884.

"Don't worry when you are not in writing condition.   If needful you can drop a postal now and then.   The best way is to come up Saturday night and have a talk.   You need a little change and mountain air.

"I am writing by this mail for Mr. and Mrs. Dielman to come at the same time.   Why would it not be a good plan to get together and talk over the completion of the story and take a sleigh ride?

"You have no idea how a little change freshens one up, and if you can spend Sunday and Monday we will all have a country frolic.   I need one myself.   I have been over-working and was very ill from nervous trouble for a few days.   I went right to Nature, tramped and rode in the open air.

So come Saturday by all means, for we all want to see you.

"Beautiful red-pine grosbeaks are feeding about the piazza like chickens.   With your powers you could go and pick them up."

"December 13, 1884.

"I should have written to you or seen you before, but I have been working hard to get the *St. Nicholas* serial well advanced.

"My heart is in the continuation of 'Nature's Serial.' Take the press generally, that book is being received remarkably well.   I tell you frankly my aim now is to prepare one of the most beautiful books that has ever been published in this country.   From what Dielman has said I have no doubt but that he'll go in with me.   I also mentioned Mr. Frost to Alden and I shall also go see Mrs. Foote.   It is possible she may be willing to take a part of the illustrations.

"But I shall be heartbroken if you cannot take the part of Hamlet in the performance.   If you will, you can make old Cro'nest and Storm King your monuments, and few will pass up or down the river without mentioning your name.

"I shall begin to make my studies in January. In the meantime it will be a summer story, although I expect to close it at Christmas, and it will be full of just such material as suits your pencil.

"I would like at least four illustrations for each number, as many full-paged as possible.

"Mrs. Roe joins me in regards to Mrs. Gibson."

"December 29, 1884.

"What can I say to you? How make you *appreciate* how greatly we *appreciate* and value your beautiful remembrance? We all went into ecstasies over the picture, which arrived in perfect safety. It should have gone into the book if I had seen it before, and had had any influence. As it is, it rounds out 'Nature's Serial' to my mind, and leaves it a past experience without alloy, except as I remember the imperfection of my own work. Can you wonder at my desire to be at work with you again some day?

"But we will leave that for the present, as you say, I living in hopes that the way will open for you to explore the Highlands with me, and to reveal their beauties to the public far better than I can. You see Nature as I do, only you interpret it to me, and make it more beautiful than the reality appears.

"I will have the picture framed as you suggest, and when you soon come to Cornwall again it will greet you from an honored place in our parlor.

"Mrs. Roe and the girls, with our guests, were as greatly pleased as myself.

"Mr. and Mrs. Drake also sent us a beautiful bit of art.   I am just delighted with the way Mr. Drake is taking hold of my *St. Nicholas* serial. I send the magazine for the year to W. H. Gibson, Jr.

"You did indeed win a victory over the ' incrementitious ' critic.   I should think he would wish to crawl into a small hole, and ' pull the hole in after him.'   Indeed you are triumphing over all your critics, and winning your rightful place. I knew this would be true years ago, because of your own truth to Nature.

"Such an experience may never come to me, probably because I do not deserve it, but I am content to make some warm friends, like the writer of the enclosed letter.   If what some of my critics say is true, a good many people who write and speak to me are awful and unnecessary liars.

"I enjoyed your triumph as greatly as if it were my own.   It was the neatest thrust under the fifth rib I ever saw, and I fear I shall never have enough Christian meekness not to enjoy seeing a fellow receive his *congé* when so well deserved. Dr. Abbott and I took part in the ' wake ' up here.

"That the coming year may be the most prosperous and happy that you and yours have ever known is the wish of your sincere friend."

"February 17, 1885.

"I have made arrangements with the best guide of the Highlands, one who knows every lake, pond, road, peak, man, woman, child, and dog in the mountains.

"We start out on our first explorations the latter part of May, when Nature is in her loveliest mood.   Say you 'll go. — I think the whole serial can be finished by October.   You and Mrs. Gibson can get excellent board at Cornwall.   Thus you will identify yourself with the Hudson as you have with New England.   I expect by then to have finished my *St. Nicholas* story and then will have the decks cleared for action.   Our regards to Mrs. Gibson and the baby."

"March 18, 1885.

"I went down to attend Mr. Cyrus Field's reception.   The trains were so delayed that I was nearly all day getting to the city.

"Well, I met Mr. Stoddard, and spent a pleasant hour with him at the Century Club on the evening of March 7th.   He asked to be introduced to me, and I remarked 'that I was surprised that he would take such a literary sinner by the hand.' He replied, 'We are a pair of them.' We chatted pleasantly a few moments in the supper-room, and then he concluded, 'Well, you are a good fellow to forgive me.'

"Some time after he asked me to go upstairs with him, and we had a smoke together. I introduced him to Colonel Michee of West Point, who is about to publish a book.

"Stoddard gave me his autograph unsolicited, written with his left hand and then backwards. I told him that I was glad he appreciated you. We had a long, merry talk, and in his conversation he said he would be very glad to have a copy of ' Nature's Serial ' with your, Dielman's, and my autographs. This request was wholly unsuggested, and he truly appeared to wish the book. Therefore, when you are at Harper's will you write your name on the fly-leaf, and then ask them to express the book to me? I will get Dielman's autograph. Altogether it was a spicy interview. I received that eulogy of your work in the Boston paper, and had said the same in substance to two or three of Harper's firm before."

"September 16, 1887.

"Your hat in the air was almost as inspiring as the sight of old Storm King.

"It was very pleasant to be welcomed, and the

day after my arrival I had to shake hands with nearly every man, woman and child, white and black, that I met.

"Mrs. Roe took cold before we started on the long trip, and has been very ill; is so yet, though she is gaining now steadily. I do not know when I can see you.

"I long for the quiet of home life. It will require a sheriff and his posse to get me out of the house again. Put down your promise to visit me and tramp the Highlands in big capitals. If you should be in town and have a spare night come up here for a smoke and talk."

"January 1, 1888.

"Thanks for your letter. It was almost as long as mine.

"I spent most of 'watch-night' on old Storm King with my children and Mr. Denton. We expected some other friends, who were detained by the storm. Coasting in a snowstorm proved very agreeable after all, especially as the road was lined with torches. The sleighs went like express-trains, and I was glad to get all safe home to the oyster supper which Mrs. Roe had ready for us as the old year took its departure.

"I have amused myself in watching old Storm King, that in the wild rain has been taking on many aspects. We have had a sort of family holiday with the few friends coming and going, and I have enjoyed all, seeing the children have a good time.

"I have had so much work on hand that I had to keep busy the greater part of each day.

"I suppose your little boy has enjoyed the season immensely. Does he still believe in Santa Claus, or have you and Mrs. Gibson, in the interest of truth (see discussion in papers), felt bound to explain that you filled his stocking with articles bought at a certain store? My little girl is still considering how in the mischief the old fellow got down the chimney.

"The sleighing is all gone. When it comes again we want you and Mrs. Gibson to take some mountain rides with us.

"Happy New Year to you all."

But other literary friends besides Mr. Hamilton Gibson were welcome guests at Edward's Cornwall home; among them were Mr. and Mrs. R. H. Stoddard, Mr. John Burroughs, Mr. Stedman, Mr. Alden, of Harper's Magazine, and Mr. Julian Hawthorne.

CHAPTER XIII

LAST BOOK — DEATH

DURING the winter of 1887–88 Edward wrote his last book, "Miss Lou," a tale of Southern life during the Civil War. In the spring he went down to Virginia to visit some scenes he wished to describe, and while there had a slight attack of neuralgia of the heart. The physician he called in ordered him to return home at once, and rest for a time.

In June he seemed to have completely recovered his health, and sent his usual invitation to the Philolethean Club of New York clergymen, who then made their eighteenth and last visit.

On the 19th of July, however, my brother complained during the day of not feeling very well, although he walked about the grounds inspecting his plants as was his custom. After dinner, in the evening, he sat in his library reading aloud from one of Nathaniel Hawthorne's works to his daughter and one of her young friends. Suddenly he paused, placed his hand over his heart, and said, "There comes that sharp pain again. I shall have to go upstairs to my wife for some remedy." But he left the room with a smile. After he had taken the remedy, which did not give relief, his wife sent in haste for a physician, who as soon as he arrived saw there was no hope of my brother's recovery. After about forty minutes of extreme agony, Edward seemed to feel relieved, rose to his feet, and attempted to cross the room, but turned quickly toward his wife with a look of surprise and joy, exclaiming, "O my God!"—then fell lifeless to the floor.

At the age of fifty, in the full vigor of manhood, his earthly career came to an end. His funeral was held in the little church at Cornwall, where he had first consecrated his life to the service of Christ, and where he and his family had worshipped for so many years.

Then he was laid to rest in the quiet graveyard on a beautiful knoll overlooking the Hudson, beside his parents and his own baby boy.

Only a little earlier in that month, and just three weeks before his death, Edward invited the Authors' Club, of which he was a member, to spend a day at his Highland home.

These lines were written in acceptance by Mr. E. C. Stedman:—

" Know'st thou the bank where ' Triumph de Gands ' are red
(My books might be were I on berries fed) ;
Where Cro'nest lowers and Hudson laughs below it,
And welcome waits each editor or poet ?
Know'st thou in fact the realm of E. P. Roe ?
    Hither, O hither, will I go."

I insert here several accounts of this last meeting, written after my brother's death by members of the Club who were present.

" I had the pleasure of meeting E. P. Roe twice. The first time was in May, 1888, at the Authors' Club in New York. It was a balmy spring evening. I had strolled into the club-rooms feeling rather lonesome among so many strangers, for I was then a new member of the Club, and, stopping at the table to admire a great basketful of apple-blossoms, I fell into conversation with a tall, fine-looking, genial-faced gentleman, who told me that he had just brought the flowers down from his farm on the Hudson for ' the boys.' I was mentally guessing who this gentleman with the noble brow and the black flowing beard could be, when some one approached and called him ' Roe.' We were soon left alone again, and I hastened to say: ' Have I the honor of speaking to E. P. Roe ?' Placing a hand on my shoulder, and bending near me with a kindly smile, he answered: ' I am E. P. Roe; and may I ask your name?' Finding that I was from the South, he seemed to be especially glad of my acquaintance, and we were soon off in a corner, seated face to face, he asking questions fast, and with the greatest interest, and I answering to the best of my ability, concerning the war history and the mountain scenery of my native State. He was particularly anxious to get at the exact social relation between the whites and blacks at the close of the war — especially the feeling of the blacks toward the whites — with a view of making correct statements in a novel that he thought of writing. Each member of the Club soon wore an appleblossom *boutonnière*, and the rooms were full of the delicate perfume of these delicious flowers. That night, on leaving the Club, I took home with me a spray of the blossoms, and put it in water, and on the following day it shed its fragrance for the pleasure of one who was then an invalid. In her name I wrote Mr. Roe a note of thanks for the flowers, and I received from him a characteristic reply. He wrote: —

" '. . . I was delighted that my hastily gathered apple-blossoms gave such pleasure to your wife. How little it costs to bestow a bit of brightness here and there, if we only think about doing it!'

"The Authors' Club was invited by Mr. and Mrs.

Roe to spend Saturday, the 16th of June, at their home near Cornwall-on-Hudson, where we were cordially promised a feast of strawberries and pleasant outdoor pastimes. The day was a perfect, a happy, and a memorable one to all who accepted the hospitality of the novelist. He met us at the river landing with a hearty hand-shake and a word of welcome for each guest, and personally conducted us to carriages which had been provided to convey us to his farmhouse, which we soon found to be an ideal home of unpretentious elegance. At luncheon our host addressed us, begging us to lay aside all formality, and get all the pleasure possible from his fruits and flowers, green grass and cooling shade. The strawberries in his patch were enormous, and each visitor to the vines in turn found Roe at his side, parting the leaves for him, and showing him where to pick the finest specimens. He was ubiquitous that day. If one strolled off among the myriad roses, and stopped to pluck a bud, he found the shapely hand of the farmer-author pulling for him a more beautiful one. If you flung yourself on the grass to dream awhile, Roe was lying down by you, telling you how happy this union of friends made him feel.

"The day wore on to sunset, when a dance, to the music of banjos, was improvised on the lawn, the banjos being played by some handsome youths in lawn-tennis attire, who, with their gayly beribboned instruments, made a pretty scene. Roe clapped his hands with delight as he moved from group to group. I heard him say, 'How often will I recall this scene! I can bring you all back here just as you are now, whenever I want to.' His wife and daughters were unceasing in gracious attentions to their guests.

"When the time for parting arrived, and the carriages were drawn up, Mr. Roe hurried from one to another of us, begging each and all not to go, assuring us of ample accommodation if we would stay over night. A few remained, and those who left did so reluctantly, some of them, I am sure, quite sorrowfully. I remember wondering at myself for being overcome by such a feeling of sadness as I waved the family a last farewell from the departing carriage. I had said good-by to the famous writer as we came down the broad steps of his vine-covered veranda, he with his arm about my waist.

"Never lived a more lovable and kindlier man than E. P. Roe; and when, soon after that golden day, I read one morning of his sudden death, my heart welled up with tears over the bereavement of that stricken household in the shadow of old Storm King; yet I felt that their grief must be illumined by the pure light that hallowed the name 'of him who uttered nothing base.'"

"ELROD BURKE."

"I fancy there are few of those active, tireless Americans, who, nevertheless, steal time from their business to read many newspapers and many books, who have heard of an association of men in New York called the Authors' Club. Authors, in their eyes, are apt to seem like inhabitants of a world apart, a world separated by a broad boundary from the sphere of average commercial labor. Authors are, as it were, abstractions; they are heard and not seen. They are heard through their books, which are the concrete essence of themselves; yet the author is, after all, an extremely concrete personage, who strives as hard as anyone for his living, and whose reward is seldom commensurate with his efforts. It is the exceptional great man of literature — the great author being a better illustration than the small one — who is lucky enough to enjoy felicity during his lifetime.

"But I did not start out here to make the old argument — which has been so often a fanciful and sentimental argument — against literature as a remunerative profession. My idea was a simple one: To assume that authors are more generally hidden from public view than almost any other class of men, and that, for this reason especially, the least important bit of gossip touching the private doings, goings, and sayings of authors interests, without question, a very large number of people. The writer of a famous novel or poem may walk the length of Broadway, yet remain absolutely a stranger to the crowd among whom he walks. A nobody of a politician passing over the same space would, I am sure, be liberally recognized as a somebody, and not the least sort of a somebody by any means. The stranger to the crowd, however, the author derives practical benefit from the 'charm of mystery.' To be at once celebrated and unknown is for him a desirable condition. His books are read. He piques curiosity. What more could he ask for?

"The Authors' Club, being merely an association of authors, is therefore somewhat outside of public view. Its peculiar distinction is that it brings together various men whom the world honors, and a few more whom the world may or may not learn to honor. It is a very modest little Club, possibly with a very large future before it. If I should praise it for one thing heartily, that would be the good fellowship which animates it and which has permitted it to thrive. Among the older members of the club — the mem-

bers who actually possess reputation — are Stod-
dard, Stedman, Curtis, Edward Eggleston, John
Hay, M. U. Conway, Mark Twain, George H.
Boker, Henry Drisler, E. P. Roe, Andrew Car-
negie, Henry James, E. L. Godkin, Parke God-
win, S. Weir Mitchell, Noah Brooks, and (in an
honorary sense) J. R. Lowell, Holmes, Whittier,
R. L. Stevenson, and Harriet Beecher Stowe.
The younger members count such names as Gilder,
Lathrop, Bunner, Boyesen, Bishop, Luska, Will
Carleton, Rutton, Matthews, McMaster, Miller,
Bronson Howard, Mabie, DeKay, Boyle O'Reilly,
Thorndike Rice, and others hardly less well
known.   Of all the men whom I just mentioned
none has a wider reading public than Edward P.
Roe, some of whose books have passed through
twenty or more editions.

"Mr. Roe is one of those authors 'who make
money,' whose writing is not thrown on the
barren soil of neglect.   His income from books
is much ampler, I believe, than the income of any
other man of letters, obtained from the same
source, in America.   Because he is so popular he
does not necessarily possess the elements of greatness.   True greatness seldom 'makes money.'
Even brilliant originality in literature has a comparatively small audience.   This is the line of
logic, since the finest writing appeals only to the

finest minds, and the latter are stray blossomings
in an oasis of respectability. It is not, in the
circumstances, difficult to explain Mr. Roe's
popularity. He tells a pleasant story with un-
affected simplicity; he is always on the side of
conservative feeling; he is eager to help men and
women, as well as to amuse them; he is, in short,
the most earnest and effective representative of
a numerous 'home gathering' that is now writing
in this country. Why, then, should he not be
popular? The bold or merely erratic genius of dis-
tinctly literary writers might not be appreciated or
comprehended by Mr. Roe's public. Even so
aggressive a person as that turbulent and pyro-
technic Frenchman, Guy de Maupassant, attacks
criticism in a way which should be a lesson to
Mr. Roe's least generous critics. Without any
kind of preconception or theory M. Maupassant
says: 'A critic should understand, distinguish,
and explain the most opposite tendencies, the
most contrary temperaments, and admit the most
adverse researches of art.' On such a broad
basis of criticism every admissible popularity
may be fairly accounted for.

" Mr. Roe, the man, is an exact counterpart, one
may say, of Mr. Roe, the author. As an author,
in the first place, he is remarkably candid. He
has been so candid, indeed, that the tendency of

certain critics to treat him disingenuously is
rather absurd.   These critics want him to write
books, apparently, which he does not propose to
write; they overlook the fact that Mr. Roe has
stated very clearly just what he desires to write.
In a preface to one of his novels he says, in effect,
that if his books are not beautiful works of art
they are at least books which tender peace and
resignation to many lives.   (I am not quoting, by
the way, but am presenting the idea which must
have been in Mr. Roe's mind when he wrote that
preface.)   There are so many clever books published nowadays which pervert the young and sen-
sitive conscience — a word not included in the
vocabulary of our 'disagreeably' artistic novelists — that it may be wise to accept Mr. Roe's
novels as good morality, if not as the best
literature.

"It is not every author who puts himself into
his books.   Drunkards have written temperance
tracts.   Blackguards have written treatises on
ideal existence.   Posing fops have railed against
the hardships which beset noble ambition.   Mr.
Roe has written the best that is in him for the
best that is in thousands of men and women.   I
have tried to indicate briefly what he is as an
author.   As a man, he is not less genial, sincere,
and agreeable than his books.   The cleverest

authors arc, as a rule, far more entertaining and astonishing in their books than in themselves. In themselves, to speak the truth, they are not likely to be either entertaining or astonishing. I should look to few of them as acceptable hosts. Mr. Roe proved himself, and proved how good a host he was, on a recent Saturday afternoon, when some thirty or forty members of the Authors' Club accepted his invitation to spend a day at his house and grounds on the historic heights of Cornwall.

"Nearly all those who accepted Mr. Roe's invitation travelled to Cornwall by water. And they were not a bad lot, taking them together. There was E. C. Stedman, for example, the most popular writer among writers, the youngest man, by all odds, for his age — fuller of the exhilaration of youth than most of his juniors by twenty years; C. C. Buel, associate editor of the *Century*, who will soon marry Miss Snow, an adopted daughter (if I am not mistaken) of 'John Paul,' otherwise known as Mr. Webb; Mr. Webb himself, wearing that contentedly placid air which he never seems to shake off, and always on time with a good story or joke; A. J. Conant, whose yarns are famous, and whose tall form swayed benignly under a huge slouch hat; Hamilton W. Mabie, the youthful and smiling editor of the *Christian*

Union; W. L. Keese, one of the few men who can speak with authority on the acting of Burton; Theodore L. De Vinne, recently returned from Europe, where he had vast trouble in keeping warm; W. H. Bishop, who has got beyond the 'promising' stage in novel writing and who will spend his summer in France; Henry Harland ('Sidney Luska'), as cheerful as his stories are sombre — just the sort of personality that does not repeat itself in literature; Raymond S. Perrin, who is kind enough to save some of his friends from disaster by presenting his first published book — price $5 — to them; W. S. Walsh, close shaven as a priest, and editor of *Lippincott's;* Noah Brooks, once upon a time presiding genius of the Lotus Club, and the author of several charming books for boys; Edward Carey, associate editor of the New York *Times;* Leonard Kip, Albert Matthews, John H. Boner, R. R. Bowker, and several representatives of the *Century's* staff.

"When this crowd of writers — numbering about thirty in all — reached Mr. Roe's home, they found Richard Henry Stoddard and Julian Hawthorne installed there. Mr. Stoddard may now be classed properly among our 'venerable' poets, although he enjoys excellent health and gets through an immense amount of work. Haw-

thorne, in a flannel shirt, with a soft red tennis
cap on his handsome head, was by far the most
picturesque figure of the group.   As to the host,
Mr. Roe, he is a man of somewhat striking presence.   He is of medium height, strongly built,
with a gravely pleasant and intelligent face; his
dark hair is brushed off a high forehead, his beard
and mustache are long and black; he has kindly
gray eyes, and his manner is that of a man who
has spent the greater part of his life in the atmosphere of home.   To do good, to help others —
that appears to be his earnest ambition.   The
notes of religion and morality dominate the note
of literature in him.   In fact, he is much less an
author than a teacher.   Once he preached from
the church pulpit, now he preaches through his
books, and he finds the latter method far more
profitable, at least, than the former.

"Mr. Roe does not confine himself, however, to
the making of such books as please the great
Philistine class.   He is an authority on the cultivation of small fruits and flowers.   What he has
written upon this interesting subject possesses
scientific value.   Upon his grounds at Cornwall
he raises some beautiful specimens of the rose,
and strawberries as large and luscious as any
found in New Jersey soil during June.   The day
selected for the authors' visit to Cornwall hap-

pened to be at the height of the strawberry season, and the manner in which these usually sedate persons made their way to Mr. Roe's strawberry bushes immediately after greeting their host reminded one of the skirmishing of boys in a melon patch. The berries, many of them with the circumference of a young tomato, were dug remorselessly from their cool shadows, while a particularly hot sun poured down upon the backs of thirty perspiring authors. But the fruit was worthy of the effort used in plucking it, for Mr. Roe has brought strawberry culture to a rare state of perfection. His berries, whether large or small, have a singularly sweet and delicate flavor; they are richly colored, and their meat is as firm as that of a ripe peach.

"Mr. Roe's grounds are quite spacious, and lie directly under the shade of Storm King. They are included in the plateau of a hill, and the scenery round about — especially in the direction of the Hudson — is wonderfully varied and picturesque. Mr. Roe's father and grandfather resided at Cornwall, and now a fourth generation of the family is identified with this lovely bit of country. The house occupied by the novelist is not the one built by his ancestors. It is a plain, old-fashioned structure, built as every similar structure should be — with a broad, breezy hall

running from end to end, thus dividing the lower
part of the house into two comfortable compart-
ments. The various rooms — and there are plenty
of them — are neatly but not pretentiously furnished, books and pictures being their chief
ornaments. On the top floor Mr. Roe has his
workshop — a long, narrow, uncarpeted room,
under a slanting roof, well ventilated, and filled
with lazy lounges and chairs, common book-
shelves, a large writing-desk, and a cabinet containing specimens of Hudson River birds. Mr.
Roe's latest hobby is to collect birds and to study
their songs. He stuffs the birds and jots down
in a note-book brief comments upon their songs.
He is endeavoring, especially, to make an exact
list of the time — to the fraction of a second — at
which each bird begins to sing in the early dawn.
'I like to get my facts from nature,' he said to
me, 'not from other men's books.'

"Mr. Roe is one of the most hospitable of men,
a fact which his thirty author-friends would have
discovered if they had not known that it was a
fact. A day seldom goes by that does not bring
him a visitor who receives a royal welcome; a
night seldom passes that does not find occupants
for his spare rooms. Whoever takes the trouble
to call upon him he is glad enough to see. If his
half-million readers could call upon him simul-

tancously they would be led cheerfully to the strawberry patch. Authors may thrive on the stones of a city because they must; but the ideal home for an author is that of E. P. Roe at Cornwall.

"GEORGE EDGAR MONTGOMERY."

"It was on one of the most delightful days of last month that Mr. Roe received in an informal way at his hillside home his fellow-craftsmen of the Authors' Club of New York.

"A rambling old house placed back from the road and perched upon one of the many hilltops that rise from the river in that most picturesque section known as the Highlands of the Hudson, Mr. Roe's home had about it that air of comfort and serenity that one would naturally imagine as the most appropriate surroundings for the author of 'Nature's Serial Story.'

"Mr. Roe was so peculiarly a companionable man that his friends were legion, and among the busy workers who constitute the Authors' Club none were more popular than he — the busiest worker of them all.

"He met us at the landing, his genial face speaking a welcome even before his voice was heard, and 'Roe! Roe! Roe!' came the greeting from his expectant guests ere they filed off the

boat. He saw that we were all comfortably be-
stowed in the numerous carriages that he had in
waiting, led the procession up the steep road that
climbed the Cornwall hills, and standing at the
foot of his veranda steps, welcomed each visitor
who 'lighted down' with his cheery smile and
his cordial hand-clasp. He turned us loose in
his strawberrry bed — that pet domain of one who
had so practically shown how it was possible to
achieve ' Success with Small Fruits; ' he loaded
us with roses — dear also to one who lived as he
did ' Near to Nature's Heart; ' and then with brief
words of hospitality that were alive, hearty and
inspiring, he bade us make free with his house
and home for the day. That we enjoyed it, every
action testified. Released from care and labor for
a day, surrounded by all the attractions that make
a June day among the Highlands doubly delightful, and made so cordially to feel ourselves at
home, enjoyment was easy, and the day was one
to be marked with a red letter by all whose good
fortune it was to have been one of that merry
party.

"Mr. Roe's Cornwall home showed the lover
of Nature and of his chosen profession. ' This
has been your inspiration here, has it not?' I
asked. ' Yes,' he replied, with a loving glance at
the quiet country landscape that we overlooked

from the broad veranda; 'here and hereabouts I have got very much of my material. I love it all.'

"The comfortable rooms of that quaint, old-fashioned house had many a touch that showed the affection for his surroundings.

"'Well, Roe,' said Stedman, ever ready with his apt quotations, 'this castle hath a pleasant seat,' and he said truly. The homelike house, the thrifty farm-lands, the verdant patches filled with fruits and flowers, and the green growths of the kitchen garden bespoke the man who added to the gentleman-farmer the practical student of the helpful products of the earth.

"'Down there,' he said, indicating one portion of his land, 'I have planted twenty-five varieties of peas. I wish to test them, to study their quality and discover which are the best for the producer to raise and which have the best flavor. I like to make these experiments.'

"A bountiful spread for the sharpened appetites of those who found in that flower-laden air an increase of desire awaited us in the cool dining and reception-rooms — thrown into one to comfortably seat so large a company — and it was a question who enjoyed it most, guests or host, for his kindly attentions and his invitation to eat and spare not gave an extra sauce to the good

things offered us.   An after-dinner ride through
the charming country thereabout, so many sec-
tions of which had been written into his characteristic stories; a siesta-like reunion beneath the
shade of the trees that dotted his ample lawn and
almost embowered his home; an oft-repeated desire that we should not go city-ward until 'the
last train;' a quiet chat as this most delightful
of hosts passed from group to group; the zest
with which the pleasant-faced wife and the son
and daughter of our host seemed to enter into his
and our enjoyment of the day — these, and the
many minor details of a June day's outing among
the historic Highlands that may not find expression here, gave to us all an experience that no
one among us would have missed, and which each
one of us will recall with peculiar and tender
memories now that the good man who made them
possible to us has dropped his unfinished work
and left us so suddenly and so unexpectedly.

"ELBRIDGE S. BROOKS."

Of the many tributes to my brother's memory
I shall here quote but two. The first is from
Julian Hawthorne and is addressed to the Editors
of the *Critic ;* the second is the resolution of sym-
pathy sent to Mrs. Roe by the members of the
Authors' Club.

"You will probably be asked to find room in your columns for many letters from the friends of E. P. Roe. I apply for admission with the others, on the ground that none of them could have loved him more that I did. The telegram which to-day told me of his death has made my own life less interesting to me. He was so good a man that no one can take his place with those who knew him. It is the simple truth that he cared for his friends more than for himself; that his greatest happiness was to see others happy; that he would have more rejoiced in the literary fame of one of his friends than in any such fame of his own winning. All his leisure was spent in making plans for the pleasure and profit of other people. I have seen him laugh with delight at the success of these plans. As I write, so many generous, sweet, noble deeds of his throng in my memory, — deeds done so unobtrusively, delicately and heartily, — that I feel the uselessness of trying to express his value and our loss. He was at once manly and childlike: manly in honor, truth, and tenderness; childlike in the simplicity that suspects no guile and practises none. He had in him that rare quality of loving sympathy that prompted sinners to bring their confessions to him, and ask help and counsel of him, — which he gave, and human love into the bargain.   Among his million readers, thousands wrote to thank him for good that his books had awakened in their souls and stimulated in their lives.   He knew the human heart, his own was so human and so great; and the vast success of his stories, however technical critics may have questioned it, was within his deserts, because it was based on this fact.   No one could have had a humbler opinion of Roe's ' art ' than he had: but an author who believes that good is stronger than evil, and that a sinner may turn from his wickedness and live, and who embodies these convictions in his stories, without a trace of cant or taint of insincerity, — such an author and man deserves a success infinitely wider and more permanent than that of the skilfulest literary mechanic: and it is to the credit of our nation that he has it."

Authors' Club, 19 West 24th Street, New York.
January 19, 1889.

Mrs. E. P. Roe,

Dear Madam — I am instructed by the General Meeting of the Authors' Club to communicate to you the following minute of a resolution that was then adopted.   It runs as follows: —

"On motion of Mr. E. C. Stedman it is unanimously resolved that by the death of Mr. E. P. Roe this club has lost a member who was en-

deared to his fellow-members by more than ordinary ties.   His kindly disposition and charm of
conversation and manner, his wide charity, made
him an always welcome companion, and though
circumstances did not admit of his frequent
attendance at its meetings, his constant interest
in the club was evinced by numerous attentions
which showed that he was present in spirit if not
in person.

"This club recalls with a sense of sorrowful
satisfaction that the last act of the late Mr. Roe
in connection with the club was the generous entertainment of its members by himself and his
wife, a few weeks before his death, at his home
at Cornwall-on-the-Hudson, an event which will
ever dwell in the grateful remembrance of those
who were present on the occasion, and in scarcely
a less degree of those members who were unable
to avail themselves of the privilege.

"At its Annual Meeting this club desires to
assure Mrs. Roe and the members of her family
of its sincere sympathy with her in the bereavement which she has sustained, to convey to her
its grateful acknowledgment of the abundant hospitality she exercised toward the club on the occasion of its visit to her home last June, and to
thank her for her generous gift of an admirable
portrait of her late husband."

I have the honor to be, Madam, with great respect,

Your faithful servant,

A. B. Starey,

Secretary Authors' Club.

CHAPTER XIV

AN ACCOUNT OF E. P. ROE'S BOOKS

A FEW more pages will be given to an account of the circumstances under which my brother's books were written, including mention of some incidents which suggested the stories.

His first novel was "Barriers Burned Away." Speaking of this venture he said at one time:—"I did not take up the writing of fiction as a means of livelihood, nor to gratify ambition. When I heard the news of the great fire in Chicago I had a passionate desire to see its houseless, homeless condition, and spent several days among the ruins and people, who found refuge wherever they could. I wandered around night and day, taking notes of all I saw, and there the plot of my story was vaguely formed."

When Edward had written about eight chapters of this book, as has been said, he read them to Dr. Field and his associate editor, Mr. J. H. Dey. He would not have been greatly surprised had they advised his throwing the manuscript into the burning grate before them, but, instead, they requested him to leave it with them for serial publication in *The Evangelist.*

In the intervals of his busy life at Highland Falls the story grew into fifty-two chapters. He wrote when and where he could, — on steamboats and trains as well as in his study, — the manuscript often being only a few pages ahead of its publication. His characters took full possession of his imagination and were very real to him.

The serial continued for a year. The next thing was to secure a publisher for the book. Mr. Dodd, senior member of the firm of Dodd, Mead, and Company, said once when questioned in reference to this subject: — "Mr. Roe brought his manuscript to us one day. We read it and made him an offer. At that time we looked upon the venture as purely experimental. Mr. Roe accepted our offer, and we announced the book. In a short time letters began to pour in upon us from people who had seen our announcement, and had also read as much of the story as had appeared in *The Evangelist*, asking when the book would be published. These letters were the first indication we had of the story's popularity, but they were very good evidence of it. An edition was issued; the book sold rapidly, and the sale since has been large and continuous."

"How about your original contract with Mr. Roe?"

"Well, as a matter of fact," said Mr. Dodd, "the original contract was destroyed and another made on a different basis by which Mr. Roe is largely the gainer. From that time we have published everything that he has written, and our relations have always been very pleasant and close."

"What is his most popular work?"

"'Barriers Burned Away' has had the largest sale. 'Without a Home' stands second on the list, and, considering the fact that it was published ten years later, is most popular. 'Opening of a Chestnut Burr' comes next; 'Near to Nature's Heart' has had a very large sale, and the others follow closely. There is not one of his novels that has not had a wide circulation."

"Have you any idea of the extent to which his books have been sold abroad?"

"All have been published in England and the colonies. Mr. Roe has in almost every instance arranged with English publishers for an authorized edition from advance sheets, and received compensation. His stories are also translated into German and French."

"Barriers" was first published in 1872. It is reverently dedicated to the memory of the author's mother, and his own words as to how it came to be written have already been quoted. Many letters were received from young men acknowledging the helpfulness of this book.

"Play and Profit in My Garden" was Edward's first book on horticulture. It was written in 1873 at Highland Falls, and was published serially in *The Christian Union*, then edited by Dr. Lyman Abbott. Reviewing the book just two years before his death, he claimed that he put into it more of his personality than into any of his other works.

It is a garden story of his own experience. The sandy knoll around the little country parsonage upon which grew only a vine or two, a few cherry trees and some common currant bushes, served as a beginning in this gardening venture. To that was added a small tract of adjoining land which was rented from a neighbor, making but two acres in all, yet the profits from this ground for one season alone amounted to two thousand dollars.

In this book he tells how his garden was stocked first with plants from the old home place, and how they brought back the sweet associations of his childhood. He speaks, too, of his pleasure in selecting new varieties for trial from the gorgeously illustrated catalogues that he received.

"What Can She Do?" was written the same

year.   Since that time numberless women have learned through the fortunes or misfortunes of life to solve this problem for themselves, but this book has found a place in many homes and by its influence has led young girls to be more helpful in the family circle as well as in the wider social spheres in which they move.

"Opening of a Chestnut Burr" (1874) suggested itself to Edward's mind while taking a walk one autumn along a wood-road on the grounds of the old homestead.   Several of the characters are drawn from life, representing some eccentric people who lived near us in our childhood.   In a "well-meanin'" man, "Daddy Inggar," we have a perfect picture of an old neighbor whom we children called "Daddy Liscomb."   He lived in a little house opposite one of our father's apple orchards, and no watch-dog could have been more faithful than was this old man in guarding our fruit from the depredations of factory boys.   He was very profane, more in his last years from habit, however, than from intentional irreverence, and sometimes when the Methodist clergyman was offering prayer in his home a sudden twinge of rheumatism would call forth a perfect volley of oaths, for which he would immediately afterward make most humble apologies.   This book Edward dedicated to his wife.

"From Jest to Earnest" (1875) is dedicated to Edward's schoolmate and college friend, Rev. A. Moss Merwin.   The story is nearly altogether imaginary, but was suggested by an actual house-party and the position of a clever hostess who was embarrassed by the necessity for making the best of an unwelcome guest.

"Near to Nature's Heart" was written at Cornwall and published in 1876 — the Centennial year. It is a Revolutionary story, and the scene is laid near ·West Point.   "Captain Molly" is of course historical, as is also the Robin Hood of the Highlands, "Claudius Smith."   But most of the incidents of the story, as well as the leading characters, are imaginary.

A few years ago I met at a seashore resort in Massachusetts a cultured gentleman who held a high position in an educational institution in that State.   He told me that his only child, Vera, was named from the heroine of "Near to Nature's Heart."   He had read all of my brother's books, but particularly enjoyed this one.   And while in California making a trip to some of the high mountain passes of the State I met a young couple living in a lonely cañon, miles from any town, whose year-old baby was called Amy, in honor, they said, of the heroine of "Nature's Serial Story."   They had no knowledge of my relationship to the author of the book.

"A Knight of the Nineteenth Century" (1877) was reverently dedicated to the memory of the writer's father. These lines form the preface : —

> " He best deserves a knightly crest
> Who slays the evils that infest
> His soul within.   If victor here,
> He soon will find a wider sphere.
> The world is cold to him who pleads ;
> The world bows low to knightly deeds."

Soon after this book was offered for sale upon the railroad trains, a young man, who had tired of the humdrum duties of his home, started West to seek adventure in the excitements of mining life. He bought a copy, read it, and was so impressed by the writer's picture of true knightly deeds that he abandoned his purpose and returned to take up the obligations he had cast aside.

"A Face Illumined" (1878). A beautiful, but discordant, face once seen at a concert-garden suggested the title and plot of this book. It interested Edward to imagine what such a countenance could express under the ennobling influence of a pure Christian life.   He says in his preface: — "The old garden and the aged man who grew young in it are not creations, but sacred memories."   It was our father who was constantly in the writer's mind as he rehearsed the conversations with Mr. Eltinge, and the enormous silver poplar that shaded the old man's front gate, the tool-house and pear tree, and the brook in which "Ida Mayhew" bathed her tear-stained face, were all drawn from originals.

"Without a Home" (1881). This book was announced two years before it was completed, for my brother studied with great care and patience the problems upon which it touches. He visited scores of tenements and station-houses, and sat day after day upon the bench with police judges. He also talked with many of the proprietors of city stores and with their employees, and his indignation was aroused when he found that in most of these establishments saleswomen were compelled to stand throughout the hot summer days, no provision being made for even an occasional rest. In regard to the victim of the opium habit in this story, he said once, "I felt from the first that Mr. Joselyn was going to ruin and I could not stop him, and suffered much with him. I also felt the death of his daughter almost as much as if she had been a member of my own family."

"Success with Small Fruits" (1881). "Dedicated to Mr. Charles Downing, a neighbor, friend, and horticulturist from whom I shall esteem it a privilege to learn in coming years, as I have in the past." Chapters from this book, appropriately illustrated, first appeared serially in *Scribner's Magazine*. But the larger scope which the book afforded gave Edward opportunity to treat the various topics more in detail. He gives many practical suggestions for the benefit of those who are interested in this subject. Nevertheless, the book is not a mere manual upon the culture of small fruits. It is happily written, and much quiet humor is to be found in its pages. To quote a brief example: — "In April the bees will prove to you that honey may be gathered even from a gooseberry bush. Indeed, gooseberries are like some ladies that we all know. In their young and blossoming days they are sweet and pink-hued, and then they grow acid, pale, and hard; but in the ripening experience of later life they become sweet again. Before they drop from their places the bees come back for honey, and find it."

Whatever may be the opinion of critics in regard to my brother's fiction, his works on horticulture are of unquestioned authority; they embody the results of carefully tested personal experiments, and for this reason have their value. In this book are given practical directions and advice that gardeners have told me were of immense service to them.

"A Day of Fate" (1880). This is a quiet love-story of a summer sojourn in the Highlands.

"His Sombre Rivals: A Story of the Civil War" (1883). In the preface he says: "The stern and prolonged conflict taught mutual respect. The men of the North were convinced that they fought Americans, and that the people on both sides were sincere and honest."

The Battle of Bull Run is simply a suggested picture, and the other war scenes are colored by the writer's own reminiscences; but concerning all technical details he consulted military men.

"A Young Girl's Wooing" (1884). Another short love-story, with the scene laid in the Catskills, where it was written.

"Nature's Serial Story" was also published in 1884, but Edward had been for several years making studies for it, at each season carefully noting his observations. He was a great lover of birds and knew exactly when each species arrived North in the spring and just when the fall migrations took place. "Song," he says elsewhere, "is the first crop I obtain, and one of the best. The robins know I am a friend of theirs, in spite of their taste for early strawberries and cherries, and when I am at work they are very sociable and familiar. One or two will light on raspberry stakes and sing and twitter almost as incessantly and intelligently as the children in their playhouse under the great oak tree.   Yet the robin's first mellow whistle in spring is a clarion call to duty, the opening note of the campaign."

He drew directly from Nature for facts, and the composition of this book gave him genuine pleasure.   He says: "My characters may seem shadows to others, but they were real to me.   I meet them still in my walks or drives, where in fancy I placed them."

"An Original Belle" (1885).   The most dramatic scenes in this book are those connected with the New York Draft Riots.   Edward was in the city one day when the riot had reached its height, and personally witnessed many of the incidents described.   Portions of the book relating to this time were submitted to the Superintendent of the Metropolitan police force for possible corrections in the statements made.

"Driven Back to Eden."   This story for children was published serially in *St. Nicholas*, in 1885.   It was lovingly dedicated to "Johnnie," his pet name for his youngest daughter.   In it my brother takes a family from a narrow city flat in a neighborhood that was respectable, but densely populated, and where the children were forced to spend much time upon the streets with very undesirable companions, to a simple country home, surrounded by garden, fields, and woods.   Here they enjoy the ideal outdoor life — perhaps as near that of the original "Eden" as can be imagined. Edward places these children among the scenes of his own boyhood and writes of experiences that are fictitious only in detail and characters.

"He Fell in Love with His Wife" (1886). A chance item in a newspaper relative to a man who had married in order to secure a competent housekeeper suggested this story, in which the hero tries a similar experiment.

"The Home Acre" (1887) first appeared serially in *Harper's Magazine*. It dwells upon the advantages and pleasures of country life, which is particularly recommended for business men as affording rest and diversion of thought after continuous mental strain. Practical hints are given as to the kind of trees to plant and how to plant them, also as to the proper cultivation of vineyards, orchards and the small fruits. He urges the advisability of teaching every boy and girl in the public schools to recognize and protect certain insects, toads, and harmless snakes that are of incalculable value in the culture of plants and fruits because of the warfare they wage against the enemies of vegetable life.

"The Earth Trembled" (1887) was written while at Santa Barbara; but, as in the case of the

Chicago fire, Edward went to Charleston before
the effects of the earthquake had been removed,
and saw the state of the city and its inhabitants
for himself. I have been told by people who
lived there at the time that my brother's descriptions of the dreadful calamity are very accurate.

"Miss Lou" (1888) was my brother's last book
and was left unfinished by his sudden death.
The inscription reads: — "In loving dedication
to 'little Miss Lou,' my youngest daughter."

CHAPTER XV

THE TABLET AND MEMORIAL ADDRESS

ON May 30th, Decoration Day of 1894, Edward's family and many of his friends were invited by the citizens of Cornwall-on-the-Hudson to be present at the dedication of a Memorial Park to be known as Roe Park, a wild spot in the rear of his home where he had been accustomed to go for recreation when his day's task was done.

Here a bronze tablet was placed upon one of the huge bowlders upon which he and his friends had often sat and rested after their long rambles.

Two of his friends, who then came from a distance to honor his memory, have since joined him in the higher mansions — Rev. Dr. Teal, of Elizabeth, New Jersey, who began his ministry at Cornwall, and was for twenty years my brother's intimate friend; and Mr. Hamilton Gibson. Both of these men were stricken down suddenly, as was my brother.

I cannot close these reminiscences better than by quoting from Dr. Lyman Abbott's eloquent

Memorial Address, given that day upon my brother's work as a writer.

"It is of the latter aspect of his life I wish to speak for a few moments only, in an endeavor to interpret his service to the great American people by his pen through literature. The chief function of the imagination is to enable us to realize actual scenes with which we are not familiar. This is an important service. It is well that you who live in these quiet and peaceful scenes should know what is the wretchedness of some of your fellow beings in the slums of New York. It is well that your sympathies should be broadened and deepened, and that you should know the sorrow, the struggle that goes on in those less favored homes. But this is not the only function of the imagination, nor its highest nor most important function. It gives us enjoyment by taking us on its wings and flying with us away from lives which otherwise would be prosaic, dull, commonplace, lives of dull routine and drudgery. But this also is not the only nor the highest use; God has given us imagination in order that we may have noble ideals set before us, and yet ideals so linked to actual life that they shall become inseparable. He has given us imagination that we may see what we

IN MEMORY OF EDWARD PAYSON ROE

"NEAR TO NATURE'S HEART"

TABLET ON BOULDER IN "ROE PARK."

may hope for, what we may endeavor to achieve — that we may be imbued with a nobler inspiration, a higher hope, and a more loving, enduring patience and perseverance. Realism, which uses imagination only to depict the actual, is not the highest form of fiction. Romanticism, which uses the imagination only to depict what is for us the unreal and impossible, is not the highest form of fiction. That fiction is the highest which by the imagination makes real to our thought the common affairs of life, and yet so blends them with noble ideals that we are able to go back into life with a larger, a nobler, and a more perfect faith.

"Now Mr. Roe's fiction has been very severely criticised, but it has been universally read. For myself I would rather minister to the higher life of ten thousand people than win the plaudits of one self-appointed critic. And his novels have been universally read because they have uniformly ministered to the higher life of the readers. He has ministered to the life not of ten thousand, or of one hundred thousand, but of thousands of thousands, for his readers in this country alone are numbered by the millions. And I venture to say that no man, woman, or child ever read through one of Mr. Roe's books and arose without being bettered by the reading, without having a clearer faith, a brighter hope, and a deeper and richer love for his fellow man. In one sense he was a realist. He made careful and painstaking study of all the events which he attempted to describe. . . . He was not a mere photographer. He saw the grandeur that there is in life. He felt the heart that beats in a woman's bosom and the heart that beats in a soldier's breast. He felt it because his own heart had known the purity of womanhood and the courage of manhood. He portrayed something of that purity, something of that courage, something of that divine manhood, because he possessed the qualities that made him a hero on the battlefield, and so made him a preacher of heroism in human life. This is the man we have come here to honor to-day; the man who by his imagination linked the real and the ideal together; the man who has enabled thousands of men and women of more prosaic nature than himself to see the beauty and the truth — in one word, the divinity — that there is in human life.

"It is fitting that you should have chosen a rural scene like this as a monument to his name; for he may be described by the title of one of his books, as the one who lived near to nature's heart. He loved these rocks, these hills. It is fitting that you should have left these woods as nature made them.   He cared more for the wild bird of the grove than for the caged bird of the parlor, more for the wild flowers than for those of the greenhouse, more for nature wild and rugged than for nature clean and shaven and dressed in the latest fashion of the landscape gardener.

"It is gratifying to see so many of all ages, of all sects, of all classes in this community gather to do honor to the memory of Mr. Roe.   But we, many as we are, are not all who are truly here. We stand as the representatives of the many thousands in this country whose hours he has beguiled, whose labors he has lightened, whose lives he has inspired, and in his name and in theirs we dedicate to the memory of Mr. Roe these rocks and trees and this rugged park and this memorial tablet now unveiled.   Time with its busy hand will by and by obscure the writing; time will by and by fell these trees and gnaw away these rocks.   Time may even obliterate the name of E. P. Roe from the memory of men; but not eternity itself shall obliterate from the kingdom of God the inspiration to the higher, nobler and diviner life which he — preacher, writer, soldier, pastor and citizen — has left in human life."